W9-AAI-325

Jess retrieved her hat and scarf from the snowman and winced when the snow inside settled on her hair.

Rufus laughed and brushed snowflakes off the length of her hair. As it had earlier, the touch of his hand stopped her dead, and the smile fell from her face as she realized that she'd let herself get too close. Again. And maybe Rufus was feeling it, too, because he hadn't moved either. His hand had come to rest on the side of her face, where she could feel a single snowflake melting on her cheekbone. She waited for Rufus to brush it away, thinking that would break the spell. But his hand didn't move. His fingers were cold, but her skin beneath them was aflame. And either he had taken a step toward her or she had moved toward him, because somehow his chest was brushing against the front of her coat, and his mouth was the only thing that she could see.

Dear Reader,

When I started writing my "snowed in" story late in 2019, I had no idea that when it came to writing this letter, a quarter of the world's population would be under lockdown, staying home to save lives during the COVID-19 emergency. I hope that by the time you are reading this the worst will have passed and we will be finding our new normal.

In this world that I created, Jess and Rufus manage to find laughter and comfort and—finally—love during their confinement, and I sincerely hope that their story will bring you the joy it brought me as I was writing it.

With love,

Ellie Darkins

Snowbound at the Manor

Ellie Darkins

HARLEQUIN

Romance

If you purchased this book without a cover you should be aware
that this book is stolen property. It was reported as "unsold and
destroyed" to the publisher, and neither the author nor the
publisher has received any payment for this "stripped book."

HARLEQUIN®

Romance™

PLEASE RECYCLE
THIS PRODUCT IS RECYCLABLE

Recycling programs
for this product may
not exist in your area.

ISBN-13: 978-1-335-55652-3

Snowbound at the Manor

Copyright © 2020 by Ellie Darkins

All rights reserved. No part of this book may be used or reproduced in
any manner whatsoever without written permission except in the case of
brief quotations embodied in critical articles and reviews.

This is a work of fiction. Names, characters, places and incidents
are either the product of the author's imagination or are used fictitiously.
Any resemblance to actual persons, living or dead, businesses,
companies, events or locales is entirely coincidental.

This edition published by arrangement with Harlequin Books S.A.

For questions and comments about the quality of this book,
please contact us at CustomerService@Harlequin.com.

Harlequin Enterprises ULC
22 Adelaide St. West, 40th Floor
Toronto, Ontario M5H 4E3, Canada
www.Harlequin.com

Printed in U.S.A.

Ellie Darkins spent her formative years devouring romance novels, and after completing her English degree decided to make a living from her love of books. As a writer and editor, she finds her work now entails dreaming up romantic proposals, hot dates with alpha males and trips to the past with dashing heroes. When she's not working, she can usually be found running around after her toddler, volunteering at her local library, or escaping all the above with a good book and a vanilla latte.

Books by Ellie Darkins

Harlequin Romance

Frozen Heart, Melting Kiss
Bound by a Baby Bump
Newborn on Her Doorstep
Holiday with the Mystery Italian
Falling for the Rebel Princess
Conveniently Engaged to the Boss
Surprise Baby for the Heir
Falling Again for Her Island Fling
Reunited by the Tycoon's Twins

Visit the Author Profile page at Harlequin.com.

For all the people working tirelessly to keep us safe and healthy

Praise for
Ellie Darkins

"All in all, this is another enjoyable, heartfelt, emotional romance from Ellie Darkins with characters you care about, and look forward to following their journey throughout the book. A thoroughly enjoyable story...which will leave you smiling, and perhaps crying a few happy tears along the way. An excellent read."

—*Goodreads* on *Falling Again for Her Island Fling*

CHAPTER ONE

JESS PULLED UP in front of the grand old manor house and shut off the engine of her rental four-by-four, suddenly wondering whether she had just made an enormous mistake. But what choice had she had? The hotel she'd booked for the conference near by would be occupied by someone else now that the research symposium was over, and she was meant to be meeting her best friend, Lara, here. If she managed to fly in from skiing in the Alps as planned, that was. She didn't have many options for finding somewhere to stay in York three days before Christmas. And driving home wasn't an option: the news was full of stories about the gridlock in the south of the country, and the impassability of even the motorways.

At least she'd had enough foresight to reserve a car well suited to Yorkshire in the winter, and so she'd driven it to their destination, deep in the moors, and now could only hope that her best friend's plane was going to be able to land, and that she'd get here before the blizzard that had suddenly taken meteorologists by surprise reached the north of the country.

She checked her phone to see if she had a message from Lara, but there was nothing. No signal. She was going to have to log on to the Wi-Fi in the house and check her messages to find out whether her friend had managed to get on a plane before the flights were all cancelled. Otherwise this was going to be a lonely weekend. And if the travel reports were to be believed, a lonely Christmas as well. Her parents' town in the south of England was already a couple of feet deep in snow, and the news was full of warnings not to try to travel.

A pre-Christmas getaway in a country manor, courtesy of her BFF's social media queen career, had seemed like the perfect way to prepare herself for the trauma of a family Christmas. And if she had fantasised about a series of events—adverse weather conditions, perhaps, a freak blizzard—making it impossible for her to return to the stultifying atmosphere at her parents' house, it had been just that—fantasy.

She hadn't really believed when she'd booked her mid-December conference and her weekend with Lara that she would end up missing Christmas with her parents for the first time.

Any time she'd contemplated not going home before, she'd imagined the heartbreak on her mum's face when she'd have to tell her, and it had been enough to kill the fantasy. At least this way she could tell her mum that there had been nothing that she could do about it. And she would go home as soon as the roads were clear.

She wasn't a monster. She was just…relieved.

The annual torture of a 'family' Christmas had been cursed ever since her sister died when Jess had been fourteen, and her sister only eleven. And then her parents' marriage had died along with her. Not that they were willing to declare it dead. The prospect of Christmas overshadowed everything, from the moment she pulled on her first black tights of the autumn, until she escaped back to her own home the day after Boxing Day. New Year had always been the beacon at the end of the holiday season, the light at the end of the tunnel that had got her through the trying week before. And Lara had always been her partner in crime, always known the most exclusive parties or hot new restaurants. Something to break her out of the sadness imposed by her parents.

She cracked open the car door and shivered. Good thing that she was kitted out for a Yorkshire winter. Her conference packing had included full thermals underneath and a long down coat on top, and she regretted nothing about her decisions. She grabbed the coat now and searched on her phone for the access instructions she'd screenshot back when she'd had phone signal.

Someone should be at the house to welcome you. However, if there's no one available to greet you, use the key safe...

Blah-blah-blah...

Well, there were no other cars or tyre tracks in the snow, so unless someone had walked here through the woods she was all alone. She shifted the leather holdall from the passenger seat of the four-by-four and ventured out of the safe warmth of the car.

The door to the house was grand and imposing, a huge arch of dark wood towering above her head. The key safe was tucked discreetly into a corner of the church-like porch, and she keyed in the code with rapidly numbing fingers.

The door opened into the hallway of all her Hogwarts dreams—dark wood panelling and exposed stone everywhere she looked. A staircase eight feet wide and gloriously uneven rose along one wall, leading to a gallery that traversed the other two sides of the hall. Decked out for Christmas, the house shone. Fairy lights wove through boughs of greenery draped along balustrades and bannisters, LED candles covered the huge sideboard. A fire was laid in an inglenook fireplace so large she could comfortably sleep in it, and at the centre a tree that must have topped twenty feet, rising through two storeys of ancient house to the rafters above. Lara had seriously undersold this place. But then, with her life of luxury goods arriving unsolicited on her doorstep in the hope of a mention on her social media channels, perhaps Lara had grown accustomed to this sort of grandeur.

Good job she was here to keep her friend down to earth, Jess reflected. She hunted down the welcome pack from the owner of the house and found a folder on a sideboard with the all-important Wi-Fi code.

She tapped it into her phone and synced her messaging app, but there was nothing from Lara yet. There was still a chance she could get here tomorrow, she supposed, though as she checked her weather app she felt a sinking sensation. The roads were bad. And getting worse by the hour. In all the excitement of missing her nightmare family Christmas, she hadn't really considered that if Lara didn't get here she would be in this huge old house— looking a little spookier, now that she thought of it—completely alone, in the middle of the Yorkshire moors.

She traipsed through to the kitchen and cracked the door of the industrial walk-in fridge. A full Christmas dinner was ready for the oven—a turkey the size of a light air-craft, with all the trimmings. The owners of the house clearly had no interest in skimping on Lara's stay. Either they had more money than they knew what to do with, or they were blowing the last of their marketing budget on the hopes of a business-changing endorsement from Lara.

Who wasn't here yet.

Given the fact that they were paying to let someone stay here over Christmas, rather than charging through the nose for it, she was going to go ahead and assume it was the latter option. Which meant if Lara didn't make it, their big gamble was a bust. She felt a twinge of sadness if that meant someone losing their livelihood.

She knew what it was like to have only a tenuous hold on your income. It wasn't as if she hadn't known going in that academia was a notoriously insecure profession. But her research into the cancer that had taken her sister from her was important enough to make it worth it.

She and every other academic in their twenties and thirties were scrambling to secure a handful of permanent, secure research positions. And then out of the blue, at the York conference, she'd landed a job offer. But one that would mean uprooting her life, and moving hundreds of miles away from her parents—which would devastate them. They had already lost one daughter, and they liked to keep her close.

But, of course, she could be massively over-thinking this and the house and the decadent contents of its fridge might be owned by some faceless venture capitalist who didn't give a damn about anything other than it turning a reasonable profit.

Eventually, as she explored the house, peeking round doorways and opening cupboards, a message from Lara pinged.

Sorry, battery died. Still at airport in Geneva. They're telling us no flights landing in UK until Boxing Day. Don't hate me? Merry Xmas?!

So, it was official. She was stranded, alone, for Christmas, in a house that had probably accumulated centuries' worth of ghosts. She looked around the place and suddenly the flickering faux candlelight, with it shadows and dark corners, was more sinister than charming.

A glance at the window confirmed that it had been snowing heavily in the time that she'd been exploring, and the light was fading fast. Even if she had been having second thoughts, and her parents' awkwardly silent Christmas had started to seem more appealing, it was too late to change her mind. She had no doubt that the roads that had seemed a little dicey a couple of hours ago would be completely impassable by now.

The overhead lights in the kitchen flickered, and she narrowed her eyes. If those ghosts were even thinking of coming out to play, she was going to have to…sit here and let them? Oh, she was an idiot, she told herself. She had walked straight into horror movie territory—willingly. And all for the sake of pretty content for Lara's social media feeds. She was every terrible millennial cliché.

A deafening peal of bells sounded at the same time as the lights cut, and she was left in darkness, the only light from the flickering candles on the sideboard. Before she had a chance to decide just how terrified she was, the bells pealed again, and she realised the sound was coming from the direction of the front door.

She turned the huge iron handle reluctantly, knowing that this was the point in the movie at which she would be yelling at the heroine not to be so stupid. As the hulking great door cracked open, a gust of snow and ice rushed at her, pricking goose bumps all over her skin. Just as she had decided that this was a terrible idea, and she should bolt the door and find the nearest duvet to hide under, a heavy weight crashed against her and took the matter out of her hands. She staggered backwards as a tall, stubbled man with reddish-brown curls sprawled on the floor at her feet and started melting snow all over the mat.

Jess stepped away from him in alarm, but really, sprawled out on the floor he didn't look all that frightening. He looked pretty vulnerable, actually. And cold. Really, really cold. He was shivering violently, huge, racking shakes coursing through his body. His jeans were soaked through above his boots, and his face was pale above the beard.

'Need…to…warm…up,' he said through chattering teeth. It was snowing hard, the temperature well below freezing. Leaving him on the doorstep would be effectively leaving him to die. She'd no choice but to let him in, but she would keep the fire irons handy, just in case. Except, he didn't seem to be moving. At least, not very effectively.

'You need a hand there?'

She took the grunt and subsequent lack of movement as a *Yes, please, I'd be ever so grateful*, slipped a hand under each armpit and heaved.

Between them, they somehow got him far enough inside that she could slam the door shut and forestall the snowdrift accumulating on the doormat. He lay on the ground, still racked by those shivers, but not otherwise moving, and she realised she was going to have to do something more proactive than just watch him die from hypothermia in front of her.

She gave him the look-over from head to toe again and realised that the wet clothes would have to go first. And the wettest part of him was his jeans. She grabbed a couple of candles from the sideboard and ran quickly to the kitchen to stick the kettle on the mercifully hot plate of the Aga. Then stopped again on her way back to light the fire in the great hall and collect the fur throws from the backs of the chairs. She had no idea if it would make a difference in a room this size, but she also had no idea whether the heating would be working with the power outage, and it would surely be better than doing nothing. When she got back to him, he was reaching for his boots with little success. She grabbed the first and pulled, nearly falling on her butt when it slid from his foot without the satisfying pop that she'd been expecting. The second went just as quickly, which left the prospect of wrestling this man—at least a foot taller and quite possibly a hundred per cent heavier than her—out of wet jeans. There was no place in this situation for either of them to fully maintain their dignity, but she didn't fancy sharing this old house with a corpse, so what choice did she have?

She closed her eyes and reached under his jacket for the button for his fly. He batted her hands away immediately, then tried to do the job himself with clumsy fingers.

'I'm sorry, but we need to get your wet clothes off you and warm you up. I'm not exactly thrilled about this either.' She pinned his arm under one knee as she tried again—eyes open this time. The button slid reluctantly through the hole and she breathed a sigh of relief as the zip slid all the way down without catching on anything. It was only when she had the jeans undone that she realised she had no idea how she was going to achieve this next part of the operation. She reached for the fabric on either side of his hips and tugged, but the trousers went nowhere, weighed down by the considerable bulk of his body.

'A little help here?' she suggested, shoving

him none too gently in the side. He lifted his hips, just enough for her to be able to pull the wet denim down to his ankles and then off completely.

CHAPTER TWO

WARM.

That was all he needed. To feel warm again. And to sleep. He was so tired. Stupid heading out into the snow rather than coming straight here. Stupid. Should have known better. Did know better.

He just needed warmth. And sleep.

The woman who'd opened the door was tucking blankets around him and muttering something about finding a phone. He tried to speak. To tell her he just needed to sleep. But the sounds that emerged didn't resemble words. Lara. Was that her name? She was gone anyway. His legs were starting to feel like they belonged to him again. If he cracked an eyelid he could see his jeans in a puddle of snow melt so he closed his eyes. Tried not to think, to remember how they got there.

The fire was burning in the grate, but it

was too far to feel the lick of the heat from its flames. He tried to sit, but found his body simply wouldn't obey. Closing his eyes again, he was blissfully heavy, sinking into the floor. He wanted so badly to give in to it. To sleep for days. But the warmth of the room was starting to clear the ice from his brain, and he remembered that sleep was bad in these situations. He tried to snap himself back to consciousness but settled on woozy.

The woman was talking in the other room but he could only hear one side of the conversation and guessed that she had called 999. No chance. The roads would be blocked for hours. No way a chopper could land. Didn't need an ambulance anyway, just needed to be closer to the fire.

She walked back into the great hall and stood looking at him. He tried to rouse the energy to sit up and tell her he was fine, but his body still didn't seem to be cooperating. He just needed to move. Even with the heavy damask curtains drawn, it was draughty by the door. But it was a good twenty feet to the hearth; he'd never make it.

She approached cautiously, like she would the grizzly bear he was sure that he resembled after his hour in the woods.

'Hey,' she said, giving him a shake, which made him wonder how good a job he'd done of waking himself up just now. 'I just spoke to 999 and they said we're completely inaccessible.'

'Don't need an ambulance.' The effort of speaking sapped him of what little energy he'd been summoning, and the urge to sleep was becoming harder to resist.

'Well, frankly, I disagree,' she said. The corner of his lips raised involuntarily. 'But that's a bit of a moot point because they're not sending one. But she said to get you as warm as I can. We need to get you closer to the fire, and you need to stick these in your armpits, apparently'—she brandished a couple of tea towels folded into heat packs.

He started to struggle against the blankets and she helped to free him; he tried not to notice when her hands brushed against his bare skin, but against the ice of his limbs they felt like fire. When he stumbled, trying to stand, she wedged herself under his arm to stop him falling, and they shuffled towards the fire. Eventually, he collapsed against a large sofa, pulling the blankets around himself.

She poked at the fire for a minute while he struggled with the blankets, but then took pity on him and pulled them up to his chin. She even found a woolly hat in the pocket of her coat and pulled that on him too. Even if he'd had the energy to put up a fight, he would have stood no chance with his arms pinned by his sides.

She dropped into the chair opposite, still not taking her eyes off him. *She thinks I'm a murderer*, he considered. And no wonder, he thought, the reality of their situation starting to hit him.

Shouldn't someone else be here? Wasn't she meant to be bringing someone with her? His brain still felt hazy on the details. But it didn't seem as if there was anyone else in the house.

'What's your name?' she asked.

'Rufus,' he said, trying to control the shivering to bite out that one word. It would feel so good now to just close his eyes and drift off. How much harm would it do, now that he was indoors and warming up?

'Rufus,' she said, and he realised he liked the sound of his name on her lips. That woke him up a bit. 'Any particular reason you were freezing to death on my doorstep?'

'My doorstep,' he said, groaning at the thought that she was keeping him talking. Keeping him awake. Bloody people on the end of the bloody phone didn't realise he was fine now. Just tired. Needed to sleep.

'Pardon me?'

He opened an eye at the surprise in her voice. She didn't know this was his house?

'My house. My door, my doorstep.' He got the feeling he was really doing a terrible job of explaining, but the cold was like cotton wool in his brain, making it impossible to think or speak clearly. If she'd just let him sleep, he was sure he would feel better.

'You're the owner of the house? Oh, good. I'm glad in a crisis we've established that it is, in fact, your doorstep. You're right— the "freezing to death" part barely needs acknowledging at all.' She looked at him for a moment, narrowing her eyes. Maybe she was wishing she'd left him out in the snow after all.

'Not planning on dying,' he tried to clarify.

She shrugged. 'And I wasn't planning on dragging a stranger into the house by his armpits and taking his trousers off.' He groaned. He didn't need reminding of that. 'What a shame that I'm the one who had to change her plans.'

He frowned again, and despite her obvious frustration he saw another hint of a smile playing around the corner of her mouth, turning up a bottom lip that was just a little fuller than the top. Her mouth bracketed by smile lines.

'Shouldn't have had to do that,' he said, hoping he sounded sincere through the shivers. 'Sorry.'

'Well, I figured a corpse on my doorstep—'

'My doorstep'

'—wouldn't be very festive. There's no way I would be out in that weather without my thermals and I felt sorry for you.'

That thought caught in his brain, clearing out some of the fog. He looked at her properly, his eyelids finally cooperating, so that his gaze could sweep her up and then down.

'You're wearing thermals?' he asked.

'I'm in Yorkshire in the middle of a blizzard.' Her hands had come to rest on her hips, and he wondered if she was angry. Mainly she seemed faintly amused by him and his frozen brain functions. 'What else would I be wearing?'

'I'm here too,' he couldn't help but point out. 'Not wearing thermals.'

She held her hand up to stop him—held his gaze too, and he couldn't look away. Seemed like moving nearer the fire must be doing the trick, because gradually the frost had been leaching from his limbs, and, with that look that had just passed between them, he was starting to feel positively warm.

'You're not even wearing trousers,' she pointed out, scuppering his argument. 'And you nearly died, which is what we're discussing here, so I get to win that one, I think.'

'Let you have it,' he said, leaning back and letting his eyes close, starting to loosen the blankets and try to locate his arms. She was going to be desperate to get rid of him, he considered. Whatever plans she'd had for the house this weekend, he was sure that he didn't feature in them. But with the snow still coming down outside, and no thaw predicted for days, she couldn't see how she was going to manage that. He wondered if she'd realised yet that they were stuck with one another until the storm had passed.

'So are you going to tell me what happened?' she asked, addressing the elephant in the room.

'Was in the woods. Got cold,' Rufus said, attempting to shrug but hampered by the many layers of blankets. 'The snow.'

'Wow, you really are so forthcoming. If it's some sort of state secret…'

'I was coming to unlock the house,' he told her, his tongue and his brain moving more easily now that the warmth of the fire was reaching deep into his chest, spreading through his body and thawing his brain. 'Hit a deer. It ran off and I tried to find it—didn't want it dying slowly. Snow came in fast. By the time I realised I was in trouble, I was closer to the house than the car.'

She looked at him for a moment, and he wondered whether she was revising her opinion of the man who had forced his way into her house. His house.

'What were you going to do with the deer?' she asked, her voice full of trepidation.

Or maybe she was thinking that he'd tracked an injured deer into the woods to get a kick out of putting it out of its misery. He dreaded to think what must be showing on his face to have given her that impression.

'You the RSPCA?'

'I'm the woman who found a random bloke on her doorstep and haven't called the police. Yet. What were you going to do with the deer?'

'My doorstep. I was going to ring the vet. Can't say I had much more of a plan than that. What were you going to do with me?'

The corner of her lip lifted in a smile again. He felt another shot of warmth at that, the thought that he could make her smile, even when he was barely making sense. Her brown eyes shone beneath a heavy dark fringe.

She looked deliberately nonchalant. 'Put you out of your misery with a handy rock and then use you to stock the freezer.'

He closed his eyes with just the barest hint of a smile on his lips. 'Seems fair.'

CHAPTER THREE

GOD, BUT THAT SMILE. Not that she could even really call it that. It was hardly dimples and sunshine. It was the deepening of the lines that bracketed his mouth from the corner of his nose into that dense beard on his chin. It was an extra crow's foot by his eye, in that split second before the lid fell shut. It was… it was a hint of something soft hiding somewhere inside this big bloke. She was intrigued.

She prodded him gently in the ribs. 'I'm meant to keep you awake.'

'I am awake,' he protested, unconvincingly.

'The eyes-open kind. You need to warm up.'

He looked over at the fire.

'I'm warm,' he said.

She shook her head. 'You're sleepy at five in the afternoon. You're staying awake until I say you can sleep.'

'You always so bossy?' he asked, and she prickled.

'I'm not bossy. I should have left you out in the snow. Now, are you waking up or am I going to have to take drastic measures?' This time, both eyes opened, just wide enough to assess her, like an unfriendly cat deciding whether she was worthy of its attention.

'Be. More. Specific.'

His tone stopped her short, and all of a sudden the central heating must have kicked in, or the fire suddenly heated up—did they do that? Because her cheeks were aflame and she absolutely refused to believe it had anything to do with old grizzly here, and the way that his whole body seemed to hum with tension as he ground out those three little words through a clenched jaw.

'I was thinking *EastEnders*,' she said, scrambling to say anything other than what she was thinking. 'Really loud. All those lovely cockney accents I'm sure you love.' He forced both eyes properly open. 'Or I could sing. I mean, I'm terrible, but I can probably manage some Christmas carols. Make it all festive in here.'

He dragged himself a little more upright,

looking decidedly more scary than he had a moment ago.

'No carols. No soaps. Nothing bloody festive. I beg you.'

'Welcome back, Ebenezer,' she said with a smile. This was too, too easy. But begging? There was something about the idea of this man begging her that she definitely liked. Deep down in her stomach where warmth was developing pretty rapidly into a heat she couldn't ignore.

'If this is your house,' she asked, trying to change the subject, 'and you look like a scared kid at their first nativity at the mention of Christmas, how did it get so pretty?'

Another grunt, another shrug. 'It's what you people want. For your feeds.' Oh, so he *did* think she was Lara. She'd wondered. But she liked having this little piece of knowledge that he didn't, and she squirrelled away her secret until it wasn't useful to her any more.

'And you like to give people what they want?' she asked, and then shook her head at herself. Why did everything she said suddenly sound so *dirty* all of a sudden? 'I mean, you're clearly Mr Customer Service here… And what do you mean by *people like me*?'

He gave a disdainful roll of his eyes. '*In-*

fluencers. Southerners. City types. You want boughs of holly and pretty candles. Picture-perfect. Substance optional.'

'Right...' she replied, taking in the look of disdain and deciding not to correct his mistake, not when it was so much fun to bait him instead.

'And of course you let these city-type southern influencers stay in your home out of the goodness of your heart. Because you're such a giver.'

A cloud crossed his face and, although pleased that her cutting remark had hit its mark, she couldn't ignore the accompanying twinge of regret that she was responsible for it.

'Need the exposure,' he said simply. 'Estate's in trouble and I'm trying to launch a business. Can't do it without social media.'

She nodded, taking in his dour expression, and decided not to prod further.

'I don't know if you care, but you totally nailed it,' she said, keeping her voice casual. 'It's beautiful in here.'

He looked around, his gaze resting on the tree in the window, the holly on the mantel and wrapped around the balcony of the gallery. The candles burning on the hearth and the fire blazing in the grate.

'Can't take credit really. Just copied what my mam used to do.'

'Used to…' Jess panicked and it must have shown in her eyes.

'It's okay. She's not dead,' he said with a bark that might have been a laugh. 'I just meant when we used to live here. Done it at the new place this year. Proper Mrs Claus.'

'Something tells me you're not exactly a grateful recipient of all her Christmas cheer.'

'What gave me away?' he asked with a long blink, his eyes sliding shut.

She aimed her foot at the centre of his ribcage and shoved.

'Eyes open. Sleep's for the weak, remember.'

He groaned. 'Was working till two this morning. Just need a quick—'

'No.' Though maybe—*maybe*—his admission of why he was so tired had her looking at him in just a slightly different light.

'How long do I have to stay awake?' he asked, pulling himself a little more upright against the sofa.

'Yeah,' she said, realising that no one had

actually given her the answer to that one, 'the operator wasn't exactly clear.'

'You didn't ask?' Rufus shot her a look of pure condescension that in other circumstances she would have given him hell for. But, given his currently defrosting state, she was going to cut him a little slack. A very little.

'I was quite busy not letting you die. Maybe I shouldn't have been so diligent. I guess you need to stay awake until you don't feel too sleepy any more.'

He groaned again. 'Oh, good. Sane *and* rational.'

'Well, it's the best I've got,' she told him, finally losing her temper. 'So if you want to call 999 and ask them, feel free. But I'm not tying up their phone lines because you want a nap.'

'We should sort out the lights,' he said after they had sat in silence for a few long minutes.

'Well, you can't blame me for the electricity being out. Pretty sure that's your department. But leave it for now. At least until you've had a chance to warm up properly. It might not even be something that can be fixed at this end. I'm guessing the snow is causing some problems out there.'

She poked at the fire for a minute while he struggled with the blankets, but then took pity on him and pulled them up to his chin. Despite the murderous look on his face, his arms were pinned by the blankets, so there wasn't much he could do about it.

She dropped onto the sofa, still not taking her eyes off him.

'What are you going to do?' he asked. 'Shouldn't you be taking pictures of something?'

Oh, he definitely thought she was Lara. And shallow and thoughtless as well, it seemed. Well, if he wanted to think the worst of her, and of Lara, then who was she to disappoint him? She whipped out her phone without thinking and snapped a shot of him, wrapped up like a cocoon, woolly hat and all.

'My followers really love authentic content. It's normally me showing my vulnerable side, but it's great that you want to get in on the act.'

'Post that and I'm turfing you out in the snow.'

'Ha, I'd like to see you try. You could barely stand up half an hour ago. I reckon I could still take you.'

His eyes narrowed and he suddenly looked

serious, as if realising for the first time that the two of them seemed to be very much stranded out here, and it would be perfectly reasonable for her to be freaking out about being trapped with a strange man.

'You know I was joking, right? You're completely safe. I give you my word.'

She examined his face as he stopped speaking. The lines around his eyes that showed genuine concern, the sudden tension she could see in his body, even through the layers of blankets and furs. He was genuinely concerned for her, and she melted, just a fraction, even against her better judgement.

'That's a pretty crappy old phone.'

She glanced down at the screen, and the grainy shot that she had managed of him wrapped in front of the fire. It had coped terribly with the low light, and the battery was looking dangerously low even though she'd plugged it in in the car on the way over here. And now of course the power was out and she had no way of charging it.

But more to the point, if she was going to reveal to Rufus that she wasn't in fact her social media starlet friend, there was going to be no better time to do it than now. His mistake had been genuine, and understandable.

And her failure to correct him so far equally understandable, given that she had had a life-threatening emergency to attend to. But if she kept it up any longer she would be moving from smudging the truth to outright lying.

If she hadn't already guessed that his business was probably riding pretty heavily on the investment that he'd made in hiring Lara, she might have been a little less forgiving of his terrible manners, but, all things considered, she knew that she had to fess up.

'Ha, so, about that…' she started, and saw a new line form between Rufus's eyebrows as he watched her. She fidgeted with her hair, tucking some longer strands behind her ear then smoothing her fringe forwards.

'Did Lara happen to mention that she was bringing a friend with her this weekend?'

The line turned into a full-on frown, and she pulled one of the sofa cushions onto her lap, crossing her legs and letting the couch cocoon her a little deeper.

'Meaning you're not Lara?'

She gave a half-smile and shrugged.

'I assumed the friend was male. Not…'

'Me?'

'Right. Of course, it was stupid of me to assume.'

'I'm not her girlfriend,' she said quickly, and then wondered why she had been so keen to clarify that particular point. 'We're friends, and we haven't hung out in a while, and we wanted…' She trailed off, not quite sure why she was explaining all this to Rufus. 'Only, I know how much Lara charges for this sort of thing, and now she's not here, and you're stuck with me and my crappy phone. And I'm sorry about that.'

It hit him in waves, she saw. She wasn't here. Lara wasn't coming. His business wasn't going to get the boost it so urgently needed. And then… She didn't know him or his business well enough to know what the end point of that chain reaction was, but, judging from his expression, it wasn't anywhere good. She shuffled to the end of the couch and let her feet drop, untucking one of the blankets that he was struggling against until his arms were free.

'You okay?'

'Yeah,' he barked, and then looked apologetic. 'I'm fine. I'll be fine. I just need to think.'

'I'll message Lara,' Jess said, trying to think the whole thing through. 'I'm sure that there must be something we can do. Even with this piece of junk.'

'I have a decent camera on my phone,' Rufus said. 'It's not bad. I use it for the marketing shots for the website.'

'Then I'm sure we can manage something. But Lara's the expert. She's been stuck in an airport for getting on for twenty-four hours and I can guarantee she's spent every single one of them coming up with a plan. All we need is some power so we can get the Wi-Fi router working.'

'I told you I should be looking at that.'

'And there is plenty of time. It's not like we have a whole lot of options other than hanging out here. You've stopped shivering,' she commented, noticing that his face was no longer deathly pale, his nose and cheeks even looking a little pink.

'The fire's good,' he said, and she wondered whether she was ever going to get anything other than monosyllables from him. She could see that he was distracted by her revelation that she wasn't Lara, and left him to his thoughts, not wanting to interrupt some pretty fierce-looking arguments he seemed to be having with himself.

'We should light more of the fires,' he

said eventually. 'The heating is mainly electric storage radiators. They'll be warm from heating up overnight, but if the power doesn't come back then tomorrow we'll be freezing. Even if the power comes back, it's hard to keep it warm with the central heating alone. You'll want a fire in the bedroom tonight.'

At that, she realised she hadn't thought about sleeping arrangements. Surely in a house this size she didn't have to worry that there wasn't room for them both. But if he had been expecting Lara and her guest to share…

'I have a sofa bed in my study,' he told her, obviously guessing the direction of her thoughts. 'I won't intrude on your use of the rest of the house. I know you're not Lara, but we had an agreement and you shouldn't worry that I won't honour it.'

Her forehead creased. Was that what he thought of her, that she was worried that she wouldn't get the sole use of this incredible place? If it hadn't been for Lara, she would never stay anywhere other than the budget hotels she put on the university's expenses for conferences. It would hardly be a hardship if he slept in one of the guest bedrooms.

'Thanks,' she said. 'But if we're both staying here, you shouldn't feel as if you have to keep to your study. It's a huge house. There's plenty of room for us both.'

He stood, emerging from the blankets like a giant moth from a chrysalis. 'It's fine. We'll work out how to deal with each other as we go along, I s'pose.'

Deal with each other. Charming.

She followed him up the staircase as he wrapped the blankets tight around his shoulders again, the heat of the fire dying away with every step.

He stopped when he reached a huge oak door halfway along the gallery, and paused, his hand reaching for the handle.

'I should probably explain...' he started, before he opened the door. 'When Lara said that she was bringing someone, I'd assumed it was a partner, and...well. Never mind. You'll see for yourself.'

He pushed open the door and Jess gasped.

More candles. More fairy lights. This time wound around the four-poster bed, right the way up to the panelled ceiling. Enormous bunches of flowers graced each bedside table and rose petals had been scattered generously across the top of the quilt. The result was overwhelmingly romantic and rendered her quite speechless.

Which was awkward, given that Rufus's social skills didn't seem to be quite up to this level of misunderstanding either.

'Did your mum do this too?' Jess asked, and then felt blood rushing to her cheeks. She looked at a bedroom decorated like this, and her reaction was to talk about his *mother*? There was something seriously wrong with her.

Like the fact that she'd spent so much of the last ten years studying and working that she hadn't spent nearly enough of it dating. She wasn't even sure if Rufus was her type. If she even had a type. But from the pink in his cheeks, he'd found her comments as wildly embarrassing as she had.

'No, this was all me.'

She knew her cheeks were glowing red and hoped that the lack of overhead lighting was hiding it. But she turned towards the fire just in case to hide her face. Pulling the matches that she'd picked up downstairs out of her pocket, she crossed to the hearth. The newspaper knots in the bottom of the grate caught light quickly, and Jess watched as the flames licked up the kindling and started creeping up the logs balanced on top.

The overhead lights came back on with a

flicker and Jess was torn between relief that
the atmosphere had just become that little bit
less atmospheric, and worry that Rufus could
now see just how red her face was.

'It would be a shame to waste all this,'
Jess said, and then quickly stumbled over
her words when she realised how that must
sound. A quick glance at Rufus's face proved
that he had taken that the really wrong way
and she backtracked frantically. 'I mean,
you've made it look beautiful, and if Lara
were here she'd be photographing the heck
out of it. Just…don't touch anything, okay?
You said you had a camera? Now would be
a good time to go and find it. Was it in your
jeans? And—' she glanced down, felt her
cheeks colour again '—maybe put on some
trousers. Do you have anything you can wear
until they dry?'

He looked down at his legs, seeming to
remember only at that moment that she had
stripped him half-naked, and then back up to
meet her eyes. 'I'll find something.' He pulled
the blankets a little tighter around himself.
'And I'll get the camera.'

'Good. I'm going to call Lara now the power's back on.'

Jess breathed a deep sigh of relief as he

left the room. She pulled her phone from her pocket and called Lara, thinking that she really needed to get this phone plugged in before they lost power again. The snow outside was showing no sign of slowing down: she needed to plan ahead if they were going to be stuck here for the foreseeable future with the power in and out.

'Jess!' Lara shouted as she picked up the phone. 'Does this mean you don't hate me? Are you okay? You didn't message me back!'

Jess laughed. Let it never be said that Lara underreacted to anything.

'I'm fine. And I don't hate you—I know you'd be here if you could be.'

'You know I would. Instead I'm in a crappy hotel without even a minibar to my name and I'm going to be stuck here until Boxing Day. Did you make it to Upton Manor? Are you okay there on your own?'

'Mmm,' Jess said, wondering where she should even start explaining what had happened since she'd arrived. 'About that. I'm not actually—speaking in the most literal sense—alone.'

'What's that supposed to mean?'

'It means...well, I guess you must have talked to Rufus, to set all this up. Right?

The owner? Well, he kind of got stuck in the snow and showed up here dying of hypothermia, and now...well, we're both pretty much stranded here.'

'Right.' The shocked silence at Lara's end of the phone was so out of character that Jess felt compelled to rush and fill it.

'And he's not wearing any trousers.'

Of course, that was the moment that Rufus chose to return. He had abandoned his coat and blankets wherever he had gone off to search for his camera, and had returned wearing jogging pants and a thick woolly jumper. More than one, in fact, by the looks of it.

'Actually, that data point appears to be incorrect,' she said into the phone, face in flames again. Was Lara going to speak again? 'Um...anyway, given that this whole arrangement was between you and Rufus, I guess you need to speak to one another to sort it out.'

She looked up at Rufus as she handed over the phone and he simply raised one eyebrow at her before saying 'Hi, Lara' as if the woman currently standing in front of him in the achingly sensual bedroom hadn't just commented on his state of undress.

Aside from the occasional *hmm* and grunt,

the conversation with Lara seemed to be entirely one-sided.

'I think we can manage that,' Rufus said at last, before handing the phone back to Jess. She looked at the screen to see that Jess had already hung up.

'Are you going to tell me what that was all about?' Jess asked.

'Lara said we need to take photos. She's refunding me her fee but said she'd be happy to share anything we can send her, and I really need this exposure. She suggested we make the most of you being here—apparently her followers like you making a cameo on her feed. It's not as good for the business as if she were here, of course, but it's better than doing nothing. Are you okay with that? The photos, I mean.'

When your best friend is an Instagram celebrity, you learned pretty early on not to mind too much having your photo taken. But surely the point here was to promote Upton Manor. Not her.

'I guess it's okay, if that's what Lara thinks will work. Are you happy? I guess you have a lot riding on Lara's promotion.'

Rufus rubbed a hand over his forehead. 'To be honest, I'm not sure. There's nothing we can do about the snow, so we just have to make the best of it.'

But he looked decidedly troubled at the thought. When he'd said earlier that the estate was in trouble, she guessed he'd really meant it.

'Got my phone,' he said, changing the subject. 'It was in my jacket pocket all along. I can sync it to Lara's account so we can upload stuff to her cloud. Lara said to get plenty of the room before you unpack. Apparently you'll make a mess.'

'Oh, that is so…' *True, actually.* Though entirely unfair for Lara to tell a stranger that. She took a few shots of the bed on his phone, knowing that they wouldn't come out well, with the light in front of them, but sometimes Lara like to use some imperfect shots in her stories—all the better for appearing hashtag-authentic, she knew.

'I found trousers,' Rufus said behind her, so out of the blue that she found herself genuinely blinking in surprise.

'Um… I noticed,' she replied, not sure what the least inappropriate response was to that statement.

'You told Lara I hadn't, and I know this is awkward. I wanted you to know I found some. We left some stuff in storage up in the attic.'

'Well, great.' What, suddenly he was the chatty one and she was all monosyllabic?

It was just… It was hard to talk. Or think. Or breathe, now that he had drawn her attention to the trousers he had found. She wasn't sure if he was aware, but the soft jersey fabric was leaving absolutely nothing to the imagination. She could see…well. *Everything.* She turned away, knowing that rational thought wasn't going to return until she did. Except everywhere she looked, she saw sex and romance. This entire room had been designed to do that. She shut her eyes and took a couple of deep breaths. She needed to think of something that would make it impossible for her to be turned on at the fact that she was snowed in at a secluded romantic break with a stranger wearing trousers that perfectly outlined his…everything.

She squeezed her eyes tight shut.

'My mother!' she said suddenly, striking gold. 'I have to call my mother and tell her I'm not going to be home for Christmas. She'll be devastated.'

'Which is a good thing?'

'Congratulations, you correctly interpreted a human facial expression.'

Good, she had her snark back. She knew what she was doing with snark. And Rufus had turned slightly, angling his body away from hers into lighting that was far less distracting.

'You don't like to go home for Christmas,' he stated, and she had to give him credit. Though it was hardly a huge leap from what she'd already told him.

'It's complicated,' she said, the adrenaline leaving her body as she started to really think how upset her mum was going to be. How sad and quiet the next few days would be for her parents without her there for them to focus on. To remind them of why they were still in a relationship that had stopped making either of them happy a long time ago. She had tried to tell them, as gently as she could, over the years that she would rather they were happy apart than miserable together, but they seemed to be determined to hold themselves to their wedding vows long after anything resembling love had left the building.

'I should leave you to it,' he said, walking towards the door. 'Call me if you need anything.'

* * *

Would she call him after she had finished talking to her parents? From the troubled look on her face, he was betting that it was going to be a painful conversation, one that would have been made a million or so times better if she were stuck here with Lara, rather than a man who didn't know how to look after his own family, never mind a stranger. But the thought of her sitting up there—upset and alone—hit him in a way he hadn't been expecting.

If the weather reports were anything to go by, it would be days until they would be able to get out of there. Even his parents' house, just a few miles away, was beyond their reach. He'd proved that by walking through the woods like the idiot that he was and nearly getting himself killed. If he'd ever needed a reminder that he wasn't sufficiently responsible to take care of anyone other than himself, then that was pretty timely. Still, he hated the thought of Jess sitting alone upstairs if she was upset. Perhaps when she was finished talking with her mum he would just knock on the door and check she was okay.

It seemed like the least he could do, all things considered. And, speaking of mothers, if he was going to be leaving an empty place setting at his parents' dinner table on Christmas Day, he supposed he was going to have to let them know. His phone started ringing, and it seemed as if his mother was psychic, on top of everything else. He accepted the video call and forced a smile.

'Rufus, love, what are you wearing on your head?' It was only as the call connected that he realised he was still wearing Jess's hat, complete with adorable furry bobble.

'All right, Mam?' he said, pulling the offending item off his head.

'Are you at Upton? I rang earlier but you didn't answer and I was starting to get worried!'

'Yeah, I'm here. It's a long story but the car didn't make it. I hit a deer.'

'Oh, my—'

'I'm fine. I'm fine. Don't mither. But I had to walk the rest of the way.' He carefully edited out the getting lost, cold and nearly dying part. 'But I made it up to the house.'

'Have you got power up there?'

'On and off. But it's on just now.'

'That's good. But I can't believe you're going to be stuck there all…'

'Mam?' he asked as her voice trailed off.

'I was going to say *alone*, until your friend joined us.'

He glanced over his shoulder and saw Jess standing in the doorway, her mouth a little O of surprise. And his mam, on the screen, eyebrows practically disappearing into her hairline.

'Oh. Yeah. Mam, this is Jess, she's one of the guests who was booked into the house for the weekend.'

The smile on his mam's face was knowing. And irritating.

'You're lucky you didn't get stuck in the snow, love. And you came on your own, did you?'

On the screen he watched as Jess approached, and pretty much wished he could disappear. Or make his mam disappear. Of course she was going to make this thing with Jess even more awkward than it already was. She lived for this kind of thing.

'Oh, my friend Lara was meant to be here too but her flight was cancelled.'

'So the two of you are stuck there together. How…unfortunate.'

If it wasn't for the enormous grin on her face he might have been able to believe her.

'I've got to go. I'll call you later. Let's see

what the weather does before we panic too much about Christmas.'

'Ah, no. You're stuck there until the New Year I'd have thought. I won't expect you until next year. Now, you two look after one another, won't you?'

His mam hung up and he pocketed his phone slowly, delaying the moment when he would have to turn and face Jess.

'That seemed to go well,' she said, and he had no choice but to turn to answer her. The fire he'd lit was sending flashes of colour into her hair, picking out hints of gold and chestnut in the deep brown. She was slight, even with the many layers she claimed to be wearing, and he had the suspicion that he could just tuck her under his arm, into his body, and surround her completely. Which he absolutely would not be doing. If the last year had taught him anything it was that he shouldn't be making himself responsible for other people, because he was in no way up to the job.

He had failed in the role so badly. He had ignored his responsibilities here for too long, off chasing his own career, a Michelin star, while his dad had been trying to keep the estate afloat—nearly killing himself in the process. And then when he finally came back—taken a look at the estate that he'd always assumed would be waiting for him when he was ready—he found that there was barely anything of it left. Most of the property and land had been sold to finance their debts, and there was only the manor and the cottage left.

He had had the chance to be a provider, a protector, and had failed at both. The fact that he was even here with Jess was complete proof of that.

'Yeah, Mam takes these things in her stride,' he said. In fact, if it hadn't been for her relentless optimism, he wasn't sure how they would have got through the last year. 'How did your call home go?'

'Not well.'

Her grimace said it all really, and he resisted the urge to wrap an arm around her shoulders.

'They'll miss you?'

'They'll miss… My sister died. Charlotte. Just before Christmas, when I was a teenager,' she said, and looked surprised at herself. 'It's a difficult time of year, and this makes it worse.'

'I'm so sorry, about your sister.'

'Thanks. It was a long time ago. But Christmas has never really got any easier.'

'I can imagine.'

He could, actually. More realistically than was comfortable. When they'd all sat vigil around his father's bedside last year, waiting to see if he would recover from his heart attack, from the massive surgery that had followed, he'd tried to picture a Christmas without his father there. Had tried to imagine how his family would work around the huge void that he would leave.

But his dad had pulled through against the odds, and the loss hadn't been him, but their home. When Rufus had taken the reins on the family finances while his dad was sick, he'd found debt after debt. The family was in financial crisis, and their biggest asset was Upton Manor. Which was far too big and too grand to be a family home when that family was in debt up to their eyeballs. So he'd convinced his mam and dad to move to the one small cottage they still owned on the estate, and he'd put the big house to work as a luxury rental, a filming location, a corporate getaway. Anything he could think of to get some money coming in. And it still wasn't enough. The bookings had been steady, but he needed them to be spectacular. And he hadn't managed to fill the key Christmas booking slot, with all the extra revenue that should have brought. So he'd gambled his whole marketing budget on Lara—and had been scuppered by the snow. Now the only option he had to get the social media exposure he needed was to make the best of Lara's suggestion that he take some photos of Jess that he could use.

He looked at her more closely now, trying to draw on what little photographic knowledge he had. The light in here was pretty, if he could find the right setting on his phone to capture it. But the composition was all wrong.

'You mind?' he asked, picking up the camera from his desk and pointing it towards the wing-backed chair by the fire.

'Me?'

'Well, no one's going to want to look at me.'

She frowned, but sat in the chair, pulling the blanket he'd abandoned off the back of it and wrapping it around her shoulders.

He looked at her objectively, tried to imagine the image popping up on someone's social media feed. The picture still needed something. He plucked a leather-bound book from the shelves behind his desk and handed it to her. Nearly there.

'Wait there,' he told her, then disappeared down to the kitchen.

He pulled together some ingredients— cream, chocolate, sugar—and picked out an old Denby cup and saucer that he thought was similar to one he'd seen on Lara's Instagram feed.

Once he'd added whipped cream, chocolate shavings and an amaretto biscuit to the hot chocolate, he snapped a couple of shots of the drink and then carried it upstairs.

He stopped in the doorway, watching Jess for a moment. She turned a page of the book and settled deeper into the chair.

Then he must have given himself away because she looked up. And maybe she was flushed from the fire, but it looked quite a lot like she was blushing.

'Good read?' he asked. He'd pulled it from the shelf without really looking but wondered now what she had been sitting here reading while he was downstairs.

'That looks amazing,' she said, obviously spotting the hot chocolate. It wasn't the only thing that did, he thought, watching her for a moment longer than was comfortable.

'Here.' He handed her the drink, and as her face lit up he snapped a quick picture with his phone.

'Don't drink it yet,' he warned, concentrating on the settings menu. He took another couple of shots, playing with the different levels to try and make the most of the light from the candles, the fire and the wall sconces.

'Okay,' he said when he was happy. And then fired off a couple more as she took her first sip, her eyes closing sensuously as she cupped the drink in her hands. There was a smudge of cream on her top lip, and he couldn't stop looking at it, until her tongue flickered out and caught it.

He was staring. Any second now she was going to look up and catch him. And he couldn't drag his gaze away.

'What?' she asked, when she finally glanced up and saw him watching her.

'Nothing.' He shook his head. 'These should sync with Lara's account. Let me know if she messages you about them.'

'This hot chocolate is seriously good,' she said, after another long sip. 'Did you make one for yourself? You should. You still need to warm up.'

'I'm okay,' he said, realising that he was.

The sleepy feeling had gone, and his limbs no longer felt heavy. Between the electric storage heating, the fires they had lit, and the heat packs Jess had shoved into his armpits, he was finally feeling warm. He owed her his life, he realised. And instead of thanking her, he had snapped and been generally unfriendly.

'I... Erm... Thank you,' he said, not sure how else to say it other than just coming out and saying it.

She startled, sloshing hot chocolate into her saucer. 'What for?'

'For dragging me in here and warming me up. Y'know...saving my life.'

'Oh, well. Having you die on me would have been really inconvenient.'

'It's a bit fuzzy, to be honest, but I have the feeling I wasn't an easy patient.'

She laughed aloud at that, and he felt it in his gut as the smile reached her eyes.

'You were an absolute pain in the butt. You were one grunt away from being dragged back out onto the doorstep.'

'Like I said...thank you.'

'Well, I guess I should thank you too,' Jess said, 'given that I was only ever Lara's plus-one, and now she's not here and you're stuck with me. I'm not sure what I would have done if I'd been here on my own.'

'You've decided I'm not a serial killer, then?'

'I think you'd be too scared of what your mum would say.'

'That's fair, actually. She liked you.'

Jess frowned. 'She hardly spoke to me.'

He shrugged. 'She did. I could tell.'

'I'm sorry you're missing Christmas at home. Who else will be there?'

'Mam. Dad. My brother and sister. Probably an elderly neighbour or some waif or stray. They tend to find someone.'

'Sounds amazing,' Jess said, looking sad.

It sounded like something she'd only seen in sentimental Christmas movies and supermarket adverts since Charlotte had died. But, from the unguardedly sappy look that Rufus was wearing, she knew that his family Christmas must be all that and more.

'And you? Do you have other siblings?'

She shook her head. 'It was just me and Charlotte. Now it's just me. And Mum and Dad.'

'That sounds…peaceful.'

'It's quiet. Not peaceful.'

'I'm sorry. I didn't mean—'

'No, it's fine. There's just an atmosphere,' she said, wondering why she was spilling this to a virtual stranger. 'They're not very happy. But they pretend to be. At Christmas. For me. It's worse.' It was also the first time she had ever said that out loud. Lara knew, of course, that she was always miserable at Christmas, but she didn't think she'd ever spelt out exactly why—she had always just assumed that she was sad about Charlotte. And she was, of course, but there was more to it than that. And she had no idea why she was telling Rufus all this now, other than the fact that she was here, with him, at what had always been the hardest part of the year.

Maybe it was the fact that he was part of the reason she wouldn't be home this year. Maybe it was seeing his mum on the phone. So happy and relaxed that it had thrown her situation into such stark contrast.

'That sounds hard,' Rufus said, his face serious. 'A lot of pressure on you.'

'It is what it is.' She shrugged. 'Though it's fair to say being stuck here instead isn't exactly the worst result I could have hoped for.'

'Did you plan it like this?' He sounded more amused than shocked.

'Hand on heart, I absolutely did not plan it. I had to be in York for a conference. When Lara asked me if I wanted to come here afterwards I told her that I had to be home for Christmas. I was meant to be driving back down on Christmas Eve.'

'You couldn't have driven down before the snow hit?'

'Not without missing my presentation at the conference. And I'd worked too hard to do that. By the time the presentation was over, the roads in the south were chaos. Coming here and hoping that Lara would make it was the only option I had.'

'And now you're stuck here with me.'

'And now I'm stuck here with you,' she confirmed, trying to remind herself that that was a bad thing. But right now she was wrapped in a blanket, in a wing-backed chair before an open fire, sipping a hot chocolate that had to have been sent straight from the gods. And on top of all that there was this tall, bearded, actually quite decent-seeming guy stuck here with her. And all that added up to—well, a pretty okay weekend, if she wanted to think about it that way.

Not that she was going to get up to anything with Rufus. No—she had been sworn off men for a long time. Her mum and dad had given her every reason to devote herself to becoming an old spinster. Because if the alternative was marriage? No, thank you.

What made it worse was that they had been happy, once. She remembered a childhood home filled with noise and parties and, well, fun. And then Charlotte had got sick, and all the joy had been drained out of them. All of them. And instead of supporting one another, her parents had started to resent each other.

Jess had thought that they would break up when it first went bad. Had hoped for it, in fact, when it became apparent years later that they had long stopped making one another happy. She had even hinted to her mother that if she was staying in the marriage for Jess's sake, that she would understand if she didn't want to do that any more. But no. They had carried on, slowly making one another more and more miserable. So if that was what became of a good marriage under stress, Jess was going to opt out before it even began, thanks for asking. Because even when you thought that you were one of the lucky ones, it could all fall apart.

So she'd kept herself busy with her studies and her work, with the occasional fling to scratch an itch when she felt lonely.

Which was why this attraction to Rufus was so...inconvenient. Because her tried and trusted instinct of steering well clear whenever she worried that she was a little too interested wasn't going to work with them stuck here alone like this.

And now that he had thawed out and was behaving like a reasonably normal human being, she had to admit to herself that she was interested. Oh, he was good looking. But there was more to it than that. It was the way that he had spoken to his mum on the phone. The concern that he had showed her when she had explained about her sister, and her lonely family Christmases. It was the fact that he had blushed, when she'd reminded him that she had taken off his jeans. There was something about the sight of a man who could dominate her in every way—taller, heavier, more solid than she was—being unable to hide that sign of vulnerability that was making her feel a little hot and bothered.

Her phone pinged, saving her from whatever dodgy direction that thought had been heading in.

Photos look good! Can't believe I'm missing out

Jess checked Lara's Instagram and there she was, curled up in the armchair. Rufus had captured her in the moment before she'd sipped the hot chocolate, with food lust in her eyes and her lips pursed into a slight pout. Not exactly subtle. She rolled her eyes and showed it to Rufus.

'Lara likes your photos,' she said. And it seemed her followers did too, because the likes were racking up quickly.

She scrolled down to read the caption:

Can't believe my best friend @Jess is curled up with this hot chocolate while I'm snowbound at the airport. So jealous, and wishing I was on our perfect Christmas getaway @UptonManor. Keep checking back for updates from Jess and Rufus. I promise it's much more interesting than where I am right now! Do you all have holiday travel disasters to share? Love and sympathy in the comments, please, friends!

Jess smiled. Lara had pitched it perfectly, of course, and she had no doubt that she would have new followers flocking to the Upton Manor page. She clicked through Lara's stories and found in-progress shots of the hot chocolate along with another shot of her by the fire, from behind this time, her profile silhouetted by the warm light from the fire.

Turned out Rufus had a pretty good eye. Between his skills with the camera, and Lara's ability to sell the setting to her readers, they might still make a success of this.

'I can't believe it,' Rufus said, staring at his phone. 'I've just got two hundred more followers. From one post alone.'

'Repost it into your stories and cross-post onto your feed,' Jess said, reading Lara's latest message. 'Respond to all the comments and use plenty of emojis. Lara's fielding as many of them as she can but apparently it's good to have your authentic voice in there too.'

Her phone chimed again. 'Good. She's happy. Says to keep the content coming. So should this have been your first Christmas away from Upton?' she asked, thinking back to something he had said earlier.

'Yeah, Dad was unwell last year so we didn't really celebrate.' She couldn't help but notice how he automatically included his family in his answer.

'I'm sorry to hear that,' Jess said, sensing pain behind Rufus's neutral expression. 'I hope he's doing better now.'

'Aye, he is, thanks. Nothing like a massive heart attack to make you embrace a healthy lifestyle.'

'Sounds like that must have been traumatic for all of you.'

'Well, for him most of all. Of course, it didn't help that... I'm sorry. Don't know why I'm telling you this.'

She frowned, looked around and pulled a footstool between her and the fire, then shot Rufus a determined look.

'Sit. Talk. We're going to be stuck here for a while. Might as well get to know each other.'

Which, from the expression on his face, seemed to be a terrifying concept. But he sat, glancing between her and the fire, and dropped his elbows to rest on his thighs.

'So your dad getting sick and leaving this place must have happened pretty close together. Were they connected?'

He nodded. 'When Dad was taken into hospital I offered to look after some admin stuff. Finances. Turned out—we didn't really have any finances. Dad hadn't let on how bad things were—thought he could fix it all himself. Which nearly killed him.'

'And you had to try and piece it all together while he was sick. Sounds like it must have been tough. And things were bad enough that they had to move out?'

'I just couldn't see any other way. There was one small cottage that they hadn't sold off yet. The tenant had just moved out and it made sense to move them over there and rent this place out instead.'

She nodded. 'Seems sensible.'

'It was the only solution that I could think of. I called the bank, explained that we had a plan and negotiated some grace on the mortgage. Same with all the other bills that we owed. I was lucky that people were generous when they heard what had happened to Dad. And then when he was well enough, we told him what I'd done.'

'And he wasn't happy?'

'He was devastated. He'd practically put himself into an early grave trying to avoid leaving the house, and then I'd come along and done it anyway.'

'Sounds like you didn't have much of a choice,' Jess countered.

'That's not the way he saw it,' Rufus said, shaking his head. 'He didn't tell me he was angry, but I knew anyway.'

'How do the others feel about it?'

'The same, I think. Gutted.'

Jess frowned, her forehead creasing. 'It wasn't your fault that you all had to move out, though. Not if there weren't any other options. You just did what you could in a difficult situation.'

Rufus shrugged. 'Dad says that he always managed to find another way. Something always came up at the last minute. He was still convinced that if he hadn't been ill then he would have worked something out.'

'Except the something that came up at the last minute this time was him getting ill from the stress. I'm sure you did the right thing,' Jess said with certainty.

'Well, I'm glad you are, because no one else is.' He shrugged. 'Apparently leaving the house has been *almost* inevitable for about three hundred years. And then I was the one to blink and give in.'

Jess scoffed. 'Doesn't sound much like giving in to me. Sounds like you were pretty bold.'

'Yes, well. I'll let you argue that one out with my dad.'

'So your dad's…okay?' she asked.

'Well, he's alive. I'm not sure that he's okay, to be honest.'

'I imagine he must feel pretty guilty.'

He frowned, causing parallel lines to appear between his eyebrows.

'What would he have to feel guilty about?'

'Well, it sounds like he worked himself into a hospital bed trying to keep you all in your home, and it wasn't enough.'

'That was my fault.'

'I don't imagine it was anyone's fault,' Jess said. 'This house is…ridiculous. I mean, it's beautiful. And amazing, and everything. But it's *enormous*. I can't imagine what it must cost to keep a place like this just watertight and warm. There's a reason the National Trust exists, and it's the fact that it's all but impossible for a private family to maintain something like this.'

Rufus shook his head, still not ready to be convinced. 'Other people manage.'

She shrugged. 'And where's the sense in comparing? Every situation is different, and from what I've heard you did well to prevent this place being sold. At least it still belongs to your family, right?'

'For now.'

'Is your dad mad at you? Because I hear you blaming yourself a lot. And not a single thing that you've said makes me think that it's your dad that thinks you're to blame.'

'He doesn't have to say anything. I just *know*.'

Jess threw her hands up. There was clearly no point arguing with him. 'Well, you're right. That seems like empirical proof. I'll use that in my next paper.'

Suddenly Rufus looked curious, and he jumped on the change of subject. 'Your next paper? You know, you never told me what you actually do.'

'You know, I know what you're doing. Nice try.'

He shrugged. 'You mean well, but I'm not sure this one can be fixed. Let's talk about you.'

She waited a beat, considering. 'Fine. But I'm warning you, you might have said all you want to, but I don't think I'm done.'

He smiled weakly. 'I'll pencil in a haranguing at a later date. Now I want to know about your work.'

He shifted on the stool, and she realised that they had been sitting in his study long enough for a couple of logs to burn down, and the dregs of her hot chocolate to go dry and grainy in the bottom of the cup.

'We can talk about me later. But we should really get the shots that Lara wanted of the house before I properly unpack and make a mess of all your hard work.'

'Right,' Rufus said, standing and brushing down his trousers self-consciously. 'Should I go and do them, or do you want to…?'

'Lara likes faces. She says they get better engagement.'

He stared at her so long she felt a strong urge to rub at her face, as if she had a smudge on her cheek or something.

'You have a nice face,' Jess said.

She wanted to die the minute that the words left her mouth. Perhaps if she went outside and just lay in the snow, her face would stop burning and she could pretend that that had never happened. Maybe. It would be worth the hypothermia. Except, Rufus's cheeks were pink again too, right there on the cheekbones, and that was such a good look on him that it was hard to regret her words. Still, she needed to backpedal.

'I just mean, we should take some shots of you too. It'll be good for the brand.'

'Fine, if you think that's what Lara wants. For the record, though, your face is nice too.'

She had just got those cheeks of hers under control, and now they were burning worse than ever. He was only thinking about the Instagram feed, she told herself. This was all just business to him, no matter how intimate it might feel being holed up together here in the snow. She uncurled herself from the chair and walked self-consciously from the study, aware that Rufus's eyes were on her as they made their way along the gallery and round to her bedroom.

'Was this your room?' she asked, trying to imagine the house as a family home, with Rufus and his brother and sister running around the empty halls, heaps of wrapping paper and abandoned packaging everywhere on Christmas morning. She'd seen enough of his mum to know it must have been full of energy and joy. And noise. A far cry from the awkward silence currently filling the great hall, where she could hear the crackle from the logs in the fireplace on the floor below.

No wonder the family were all missing this

place. That Rufus was mourning what he had lost. She knew as well as anyone how hard it was when big changes hit your family. When you suddenly had to adjust to a new normal, when you had been perfectly happy with the old one.

She opened the door to her room and was hit by warmth from the fire, which had been burning away behind the closed door while they were in the study. The décor, unsurprisingly, seemed no less over-the-top after an hour away from it, and she tried to imagine what she and Lara would have made of it had she got her flight before the snow had set in. They would have been doubled up with laughter, she imagined, at the thought of their plans for a pyjama-and Scrabble-heavy weekend being mistaken for a debauched couple of nights involving rose petals and champagne. There was no doubt it would make for some pretty content for the Instagram feed, though. She'd picked up Rufus's phone in the study and fired off a couple of shots now, capturing the heart of petals on the bed and the champagne glasses on the side table. A tall cheval mirror was reflecting the fire from the other side of the room and she crossed to stand in front of it, wondering what Lara would make of her very hashtag-authentic outfit of thermal leggings, worn-in boots and layers of knitwear that no one would mistake for cashmere.

'I really don't know what to do with all this,' Jess said, contemplating the mass of rose petals that she'd gathered into a pile.

'Here.' Rufus snatched up a crystal bowl from the dark wood sideboard on the other side of the room and crossed to the bed. They scooped handfuls of petals into the bowl, until there were just a few strays on the pillows that Jess stretched to pick up.

'These smell beautiful,' Jess said, picking up the bowl and giving it a long sniff. 'Mind if I keep them up here?'

'If you want,' Rufus replied, dropping down to sit on the edge of the bed, but then standing up, looking uncomfortable.

'Sorry,' he said. 'Sometimes it's hard to remember I don't live here any more.'

'Was this your room?'

He shook his head. 'No, my parents had this one. Mine was far less grand—they stuck us up in the attic once we were old enough to be out of earshot.'

Jess smiled. 'Sounds very *Boy's Own*.'

'I don't know about that. My sister was up

there with us. They're still bedrooms—you can take a look if you want.'

'I'd like that, maybe once the house warms up a bit. I'm not sure that I want to leave the fire. And you should sit, Rufus, if you want. You have more right to be here than I do. It's not fair that you should feel uncomfortable.'

'You're a guest,' he said.

'Well, and so are you, sort of, if it makes you feel better. I dragged you in from the cold and saved your life, which means I get to decide what to do with it. And right now I really think you should relax.'

'Is that what you and Lara were planning on doing?'

She nodded. 'Yep. Our plan for the weekend was pyjamas, movies, Scrabble.'

'Scrabble?'

'Lara's a fiend.'

'How about you? Maybe I'll let you beat me later.'

'Let me?' She raised an eyebrow. 'Wow. You don't know who you're messing with.'

The buzz of her phone in her pocket stopped that intense look from becoming uncomfortably long, and she tapped on Lara's message. She'd cropped one of the mirror shots, and Jess realised for the first time that she had captured Rufus in the glass behind her, and he was looking at her with an expression she could only describe as heated. She zoomed in on his face a little further, and then nearly dropped her phone in panic as he came to stand beside her.

'More from Lara?'

'Uh, yeah. She's happy with the shots from in here.'

'Can I see?'

If she could have thought of a single good reason to say no, she would have done. But these photos were the key to saving his family home and his business. They were the whole reason that she was here, and she couldn't think how to avoid him seeing them. She handed the phone over, surreptitiously tapping the back key so that he couldn't see how close a close-up she'd made it.

'Oh,' he said, his eyebrows furrowing together. 'I didn't realise you'd taken that.'

'I didn't realise you were in it,' she told him honestly.

And then, just as they were both staring at the phone, a message popped up from Lara. Three flame emojis. Which everyone knew translated as *Oh, my goodness, check out the scorching sexual chemistry*. Jess rolled her eyes. Lara's timing was impossibly, perfectly terrible.

She wrote back.

You're right. The log fires are our only source of heat. Well spotted.

And then she pocketed her phone before her friend could heap any more embarrassment on her.

'Does she want us to take any more tonight?' Rufus asked.

Jess made an executive decision.

'Probably best to wait for natural light. These are good for now for her stories, but she'll want them better lit for the main grid. So I'm going to say we're off duty.'

'In that case…are you hungry?'

She tried to think back to the last time that she had eaten and could only think of the nondescript beige food that she'd found at the hotel's continental breakfast buffet. And suddenly she was ravenous.

'I'm starving. Shall we raid the fridge?'

'Did Lara mention that catering is…kind of my thing? I'm a chef, and the food's included in the weekend. In fact, we should probably get some pictures of that too.'

Rufus pulled a giant tray of lasagne from the fridge and stuck it in the Aga, then dug around in the fridge for salad and olives and other things to pick at while they waited for it to warm up.

'What would you be doing, if you weren't here?' she asked on a whim, thinking about her parents, wondering whether they were home alone together on a Saturday night, sitting silently in front of the television and wishing they were anywhere else.

'Saturday night before Christmas? In my old life, I'd be at work. No chance of being out of the kitchen before midnight. And then back here for booze, board games, snacks with whoever was still awake. An argument with my brother, probably. The traditional Taylor night in.'

'I can't decide whether that sounds terrible or wonderful.'

Rufus lifted his shoulders, then let them drop. 'If it helps, it's usually both. What about you? What would you be doing if you were with your family?'

She had to suppress a shudder. 'Forced conversation. Awkward silences. Trying to subtly convince my parents to separate.'

He watched her for a long moment as she

realised she'd been far more honest than she'd intended.

'I'm sorry,' Rufus said, his voice so full of empathy that she felt the warmth of it in her bones.

'They never recovered,' she said, wondering where this need to talk was coming from. 'They were both so…devastated when my sister died. And they could—they *should*—have turned to each other. To support one another. To get through it. But it was like…' She hesitated. Realised there was a tear in the corner of her eye and swiped it away before it could betray her. 'They both just stopped talking. As if that would somehow change something.' She shook her head. 'I'm sorry. I really don't know why I'm telling you this.'

'Because you're stranded in my house at Christmas instead of being with them?'

She shrugged. 'Maybe. Did your family rally round when your dad was sick?'

'We all had to pitch in. Between that and me moving back here and packing up the house it's been a full-on year.' And it had brought them all together, that much was clear from the way that he spoke about them.

And that was the thing: some families, some couples, survived these traumas. Others didn't. And until you were in the middle of it—in a brightly lit hospital corridor in the middle of the night, hearing terrible news and wondering what your life was going to be now—you didn't know which way it was going to fall.

There were plenty of people—her parents included—who thought they were in a happy, stable marriage. And then when the worst happened, they discovered that that wasn't enough.

Which was precisely why Jess had steered clear of anything remotely resembling a serious relationship her entire adult life. What was the point if even something you thought was perfect could disintegrate in the space of a heartbeat? Or the space where a heartbeat should have been.

'Right. Enough wallowing—'

'It's okay to wallow if you feel sad,' Rufus said gently.

'Enough wallowing,' she repeated. 'Now you've made me realise how hungry I am, we have to eat.'

He pulled the lasagne out of the Aga and reached for a serving spoon without looking up. All muscle memory, she realised. He'd grown up in this kitchen. Was a part of it.

They took their steaming plates of food to the huge table in the centre of the kitchen and she plonked herself onto a bench opposite Rufus, and Jess was struck by how intimate this was. She couldn't remember the last time she'd had dinner alone with a man.

These days her social life was mainly messaging Lara and the occasional departmental social. And she'd never really minded that before. But, sitting here with Rufus, trying to remember how to hold a conversation that didn't revolve around work, she realised that this was an adult life skill she really should have mastered by now.

'You asked earlier what I do. I'm a researcher, looking at genetic links in childhood cancers. It's such a cliché, but after we lost Charlotte I was just drawn to it.'

Rufus looked surprised. 'You want to help other families. It's not a cliché. It's—I don't know. Remarkable. Isn't it painful? The constant reminder?'

She thought about his question. 'It's always painful. At least this way it's doing some good.'

He narrowed his eyes, as if trying to slot these pieces into the puzzle picture he had of her. One that had somehow got stuck on his mistaken assumption that she was Lara.

'How did you and Lara meet?' Rufus asked, sparing her the trauma of trying to remember how to converse like a normal human being.

'Oh, university. We were flatmates and she's never really got rid of me.'

'And the pre-Christmas thing is a one-off?'

'Nope. Annual event. We used to try and get so drunk that it would numb me right through the big day. Last couple of years have been more just a massive inoculation of moral support.'

He smiled. 'She sounds like a good friend.'

'She's the best.'

'I'm sorry I was… I don't know…rude about her earlier. When I thought you were her.'

'Well, you were rude, but I accept your apology. I do wonder though why you invited her here at all if you think so little of what she does.'

'No, I don't.' He clocked her doubtful expression and doubled down. 'I can understand why you think that after what I said. But I respect the work she does. I know she's very good at it. I just don't want to see my home reduced to *content*. I don't like having to stage "real life", so that people can come here and make-believe my old life for the weekend.'

She nodded. 'You're mourning this place too,' she observed. 'And I don't blame you. It's beautiful. I would have been heartbroken to leave too.'

'It's not that it's beautiful,' he said, an edge to his voice. 'That's the problem. That's all social media is going to show, and it's only a fraction of what this place is. What it means to me.'

'Then tell me. Help me understand.'

'It's…it's where I belong. It's where my brother belongs. And my sister. And my parents. It's the place where I feel most like me in the whole world—I thought that it would always be here. Instagram doesn't care about that.'

'Then make it care.'

'And how do I do that?'

'I don't know. That's Lara's department. But you have an opportunity here. Lara has a huge following. Millions of people view her posts, and you're the one with the camera. So don't show them the gloss. Show them what this house means to you. Show them things that no one else would never see because they didn't know to look for them. Show them what makes this a home, not just another luxury rental.'

He stared at her, and she started to shift uncomfortably. If she'd gone too far, she'd just created an atmosphere in a house that neither of them could escape from. She might as well have gone home for Christmas and put up with an atmosphere she at least knew and understood.

He nodded slowly, and she could see that hint of a smile turn up the corner of his mouth. 'I think I can do that. I know I can. But I'm going to need your help.'

CHAPTER FOUR

RUFUS LOOKED AT the clock on the kitchen wall again. Five minutes past nine. When he'd said goodnight to Jess last night she'd asked him to give her a shout if she slept past nine—her phone had died, and she couldn't be sure it would charge overnight, so she couldn't set an alarm.

He poured two cups of coffee and glanced at the clock again. Why was he hesitating? She'd specifically asked him to wake her, but somehow the thought of taking coffee to her in bed of a morning felt so…intimate. And the thought of sharing something like that with Jess was intimidating. Because he knew there was something between them. It had been obvious from the moment his head had cleared yesterday and he'd found himself sharing the house with a woman who'd dragged him in from the snow, saved his life, and then kept up a steady stream of snark in the hours afterwards. And he'd found it pretty irresistible. Seeing her curled up in the chair by the fire in the study, he had found it hard to hide just how irresistible. But, regardless of what he was feeling, he knew that he wouldn't act on it.

Some time in the year that his father had been recuperating, he'd decided that he wasn't going to be responsible for another family. He'd had a go at acting as provider, and he'd messed up, so badly that it had uprooted his entire family from the home that they'd loved for generations. and for what? His ambition? A job that he'd had to leave anyway?

He was at least smart enough to know that he should never be in the position of being responsible for other people's happiness.

So he was going to knock on her door, deliver strong coffee, and retreat, ideally without making eye contact.

And after that his focus was going to be on his camera, and on showing the world Upton Manor as it was truly meant to be seen.

He carried the coffee up the stairs and across the gallery, listening out for any sound that would indicate that Jess was awake and he was off the hook. But the house was silent, in a way that he never remembered it being before the moving trucks had turned up. He knocked on the door gently and then more loudly, waiting for a shout of 'I'm up' from the other side of the door. Which never came.

He opened the door a crack and peered in, but the heavy curtains were pulled across and he could barely see anything in the darkened room. 'Jess,' he said, but her name came out as a croak. He called her again, his voice louder this time, pushing open the door to allow more light to spill in.

Jess sat bolt upright in bed with a scream, and Rufus jumped, splashing hot coffee on his chest in the process. He had no choice but to set the cups down on the sideboard just inside the door.

'Hey, it's me. It's Rufus,' he said as he stepped through the door, holding up his now empty hands. 'You asked me to wake you up.'

'I… I did. I'm sorry for screaming; didn't know where I was for a second. Is that coffee?'

'Yeah.' For want of anything better to do, he picked up both the cups, carried them over to the bed and handed one to Jess. She took a long sip, and he winced, knowing just how hot it was.

'Is it working?' he asked as she ventured another, more cautious, sip.

'I do not want to be awake right now.'

'You know, I'm not sure I would have agreed to this whole wake-up call thing if I'd known you were so aggro in the morning.'

'Sorry. And thanks. It would only have been worse if I'd slept any later. I owe you one.'

She shifted on the bed and he hesitated, not sure if it was an invitation, but then her head dropped back on the pillows and her eyes drifted closed and he knew he needed to stick around for a bit if she was going to stay awake.

He sat on the edge of the bed, and the movement of the mattress woke her again.

'I wasn't asleep.'

'Glad we cleared that up.'

Her hair was smooshed into some sort of asymmetrical beehive, and her face still had creases from the pillow, and the whole look was so utterly adorable that he had to look away because it was absolutely not part of his plan to adore her in any way.

As if she'd sensed the direction of his thoughts, she lifted a hand to her hair, patted it a few times from different angles and rolled her eyes.

She sat up properly, resting her arms on bent knees as she blew on her coffee.

'Do we have exciting plans for today?' Jess asked.

'I'm going to take more photos for Lara. I was going to wrap up and head out into the snow. Make the most of the sun being out for a bit.'

'Back on the horse?'

'Something like that. You should come with me—if you see me wandering into the woods after a deer you can yell at me not to be such an idiot.'

'Noted. Seriously, though.' She lowered her coffee and gave him a stern look. 'Are you feeling okay? Because you could just sit by the fire today and carry on warming up.'

'I'm fine. I mean it.' He hated people fussing over him. It was bad enough that he had let his family down, but he was at least capable of taking care of himself. Most of the time.

He glanced back at Jess—the creases were fading from her cheeks, her hair had settled around her shoulders and her eyes fell shut every time she took a sip from the cup.

'Right,' she said at last, draining the last of the coffee and straightening her spine with resolve. 'I'm awake. I'm alive. Thanks so much for the coffee. Shall I meet you downstairs in five and we can head out?'

He dragged his eyes away from her and headed for the door, pulling it closed behind him when he heard her feet hit the floor and he knew she wasn't going back to sleep.

Jess scrambled out of bed and rummaged in her bag for her thick woollen socks and a couple of jumpers. After she'd asked Rufus last night to wake her if she accidentally slept in—post-conference fatigue had a habit of messing up her body clock—she'd pulled on tartan flannel PJs, making sure there was nothing on show if he came in to wake her this morning. And that she didn't freeze half to death in the night.

After a chilly—and necessarily quick—stint in the bathroom, she pulled on thermals, trousers, layers of knitwear, and dug her snow boots from the bottom of her bag. If they were going out in the snow then she was going prepared. She could see from the window that a few more inches had fallen overnight, and Rufus had been the proof yesterday of how important it was to be careful out there.

She bounded down the staircase into the great hall, where Rufus had swept out the remains of yesterday's fire and laid a new one with logs from the basket by the hearth. The power had stayed on overnight, which meant the electric heaters were warm, but they were going to need more wood to get them through the next few days if the supply couldn't be relied upon. The wall sconces flickered, a timely reminder that they couldn't depend on modern technology to see them through the crisis when the weather was so extreme.

Rufus appeared in the doorway that led down to the kitchen, piece of toast in hand.

'Did the lights just flicker in here?'

'Yeah, I think so,' she said, glancing up. 'Do you think we'll lose power again?'

'Not if I can help it,' he said, a collection of frown lines gathering on his forehead. If a power line came down somewhere, or something else happened on the grid, she wasn't sure what he was going to do about it. But from the sternness of his expression this wasn't the moment to mention it.

'Do you want toast?' he asked, gesturing

old phone could capture something beautiful.

tty,' Rufus said, coming up behind her ooking at her phone screen. 'But Lara faces, remember.' He lifted his phone ired off a shot before she had a chance agree.

etty,' he said again, looking at the photo, e he had captured her in profile, the light ing from the cobweb making a bokeh ef- behind her. He was probably just compli- ting himself on the composition, Jess told self, feeling colour rising on her cheeks. It ild be so much more convenient if he was. Uh, nice one,' she said, before stomping through the snow, glorying in each crunch the snow underfoot as she crossed the drive d turned back to look at the house. 'It's like mething out of a fairy tale,' Jess said as ufus came to stand beside her and followed er gaze to the big old house.

'That's the problem, though,' he said. 'It ooks like a fairy tale, and people don't be- ieve that it's real. That's it's warm and has a personality of its own. That's what I want to show people.'

She took a picture of him looking up at the house, the yearning in his face for his home.

with his own slice, and Jess's stomach rum- bled an enthusiastic yes. She followed him through to the kitchen and found a rack full of toast and sticky jars of jam and honey. She slathered a slice with butter and honey while Rufus filled a couple of Thermos mugs with freshly brewed coffee.

'Are you planning a major expedition?' she asked with eyebrows raised.

'You've got your thermals, I have coffee. Let's try no one getting hypothermia today.'

'I'm fine with that part. I'm mainly plan- ning half-hour stints in the outdoors broken up by long stretches on the sofa with a book. We're just taking a few photos, right?'

'Right. And I should probably get some more logs out of the woodstore. But you're welcome to stay inside if you want.'

'No! I want to come out and play. But I will not be staying out so long that hypo- thermia measures will have to be taken. Just to be clear.'

'Crystal clear. The coffee is an added bonus, not a life-saving measure.'

'Then hand it over,' she said with a smile.

As she took the cup from him, her fingers brushed against his wrist, and she felt him freeze at the exact same moment she did. He looked up and found his gaze on her face, and she was reminded of that spark she'd felt yesterday, when they'd been cocooned in a candlelit house, cut off from the world. But it seemed that spark hadn't died when the fires had burned down to embers last night. She'd half wondered if it had been summoned by the sheer quantity of fairy lights, but here they were in bright daylight and it was definitely still there.

She drew her hand back, because as delicious as sparks could be, they had to be handled with care. Sparks, all too often, led to feelings. Feelings led to relationships, and relationships led to heartache. She'd experienced and witnessed it enough in her life, and had precisely zero interest in exposing herself to any more.

She'd acted on sparks before. In controlled circumstances, when she'd been absolutely certain that she knew how she was getting in and when she was going to be getting out. Right now, these circumstances were anything but controlled. They'd been thrown together, entirely unexpectedly, with lashings of Christmas and adverse weather conditions thrown in for extra pressure. So she was going to back the heck away, and pretend

that she hadn't noticed an in the first place.

'I need to get my coat an she'd last seen on his hea tunately he produced it fro his jacket without commen it straight onto her head. 'F ready.'

She pulled aside the heavy that covered the front door and diate blast of cold air from the ing their way around the ancie When she opened it, snow had in the porch, and she was glad boots as she crunched slowly out footing to see if she was going t slip.

But the snow was deliciously sof dery underfoot, and she felt a hu spread across her face as she too great expanse of white all around across the landscape, as far as she co was virgin, untouched snow. The tre heavy with it, icicles hung from the en to the porch, and a spider's web glis with tiny crystals. She grabbed her from her pocket and snapped a couple o tures, the natural light meaning that eve

junky
quite
'Pre
and l
wants
and f
to dis
'P
when
glint
fect
me
her
wo

of
of
a
s
R
h

Lara was going to eat this up, she thought, uploading her last few photos to her friend's cloud account.

'Come on,' Rufus said. 'I just want to check there's nothing I can do about the power out here, check the place is secure. Then I'll get some more logs from the outhouse and we can get you back in by the fire. That sound okay?'

'That sounds…efficient,' she answered. 'Um, any chance of, say, some fun?'

He frowned. 'You were all *I'm only staying out for half an hour…*'

'Precisely. I want to have half an hour of fun. Taking photos. I heard no snowmen, snowballs or snow angels in your plan. This is a shocking oversight.'

'You think I want to lie in the snow after yesterday?'

'Good point. You are exempt from snow angels. You are not exempt from the rest of it. I thought you wanted to show that this place has personality. That might involve, you know, *you* having a personality.'

'I'm trying really hard to see how that can be anything but an insult. I'm coming up with nothing.'

'I'm just saying that this house doesn't have

a personality all on its own. You love it because you grew up here with the people that you love. You're going to have to show some of that if you want other people to see it.'

'Fine. I get it. There will be fun in the snow. Just as soon as I've checked the fuse box.'

'I'm very glad to hear it. Now—snowman. I'm going to warn you—I have a problem with half-arsed. I'm expecting great things of myself, and of you.'

He raised an eyebrow. 'Are you this competitive about everything?'

'Generally, yes.'

'Then I'm glad we never got to Scrabble last night. I suspect you would have been vicious.'

She shrugged. 'I guess you'll never know if you're too chicken to try. If your masculinity is too fragile to lose to a girl, there's not much hope for you.'

'Fragile…wow.'

Jess shrugged, trying to hide a smile. 'I guess you'll just have to prove it.'

'You're on. Scrabble later, snowman competition now.'

She grinned, unable to resist a challenge. Or that look on his face, apparently. 'Com-

petitive snowman-making. You do know how
to make a girl happy.'

She started gathering snow in a pile around
her, pushing it together to form a ball. Her
gloves were soaked through within seconds,
and her fingers started to sting as the cold set
in. But she glanced over at Rufus and smiled
at the fierce concentration on his face as he
piled snow on top of snow until he had a pile
nearly to his hips. She took a couple of photos
while he was looking the other way, getting
bright blue skies and clear winter sun in the
background. On a summer's day she'd look
at that sky and expect to bake beneath it. But
apparently all it meant for them for the next
few days were temperatures that never crept
above zero.

The main roads would be gritted and
cleared pretty soon, she guessed. But out here
in the wilds of the moors at the end of a winding lane, they just had to wait for the thaw.

And try not to get into trouble in the mean-
time, she reminded herself, realising she had
been staring at Rufus's arse for way longer
than could be considered appropriate. Especially for someone who had sworn to herself,
at least once already this morning, that she

was steering well clear of the chemistry she had to acknowledge existed between them.

Rufus glanced over his shoulder, and she was glad she'd already shifted her gaze upwards and hadn't been caught perving on him. That would have been awkward.

'You've slowed down,' Rufus commented. 'You ready to go in and warm up?'

Jess rolled her eyes. 'Nice try.' With that she started to roll the snowman's body around, gathering more snow as she went, until it was as high as her waist. She made a smaller ball for the head, added her hat and scarf, and glanced over to check out how the competition was getting on.

Rufus had built a rather austere-looking snowman and was currently carving out arm shapes. Jess came to stand beside him and grinned at the concentration on Rufus's face.

'Okay, you make a good snowman,' she acknowledged. 'I'll give you that.'

He turned and smiled at her, and it was so unexpected that it caught her off guard, disarming her with its easy openness. Woah. She clearly needed much better defences. She picked up her phone and took a couple more pictures of the snowman. Everything seemed that little bit safer through the lens of a camera.

Rufus slung an arm around the snowman's really-quite-impressive shoulder and took a selfie. Jess leaned into the shot from the other side and grinned at the lens as Rufus took another couple. He came round to show her, and she grinned at the result.

'Nice work. He's very handsome,' she told him. 'But your nose is red. You look cold.'

'Yours is red too. And don't think I didn't notice that your hands are freezing.'

'I wasn't hypothermic yesterday. We should go inside.'

Rufus shook his head. 'I haven't checked the fuses. Or fetched in the wood.'

'They'll still be there in an hour,' she told him. 'Anyway, I finished my coffee ages ago and my caffeine levels are slipping dangerously low. It's my turn to put the kettle on.'

Rufus hesitated, so she pulled out the big guns. 'I'm not going inside until you do. So if you want me to warm up, you're going to have to go in too.'

'Fine. You're stubborn. I'll go in, we'll make coffee and I'll head back out soon.'

Jess nodded. 'Acceptable.' She retrieved her hat and scarf from the snowman, and winced when the snow inside the hat settled on her head. Rufus laughed and brushed snowflakes off the length of her hair. As it had earlier, the touch of his hand stopped her dead, and the smile fell from her face as she realised that she'd let herself get too close. Again. And maybe Rufus was feeling it too, because he hadn't moved either. His hand had come to rest on the side of her face, where she could feel a single snowflake melting on her cheekbone. She waited for Rufus to brush it away, thinking that would break the spell. But his hand didn't move. His fingers were cold, but her skin beneath them was aflame. And either he had taken a step towards her or she had moved towards him, because somehow his chest was brushing against the front of her coat, and his mouth was the only thing that she could see.

And his hand was cupping her cheek—and how was hers on his waist?—and their frozen breath was mixing between them.

The touch of his cold lips on hers shocked her out of her paralysis and she took a decisive step back.

'I'm sorry,' Rufus said immediately.

'No need to apologise,' Jess said, trying to school her features into something neutral. 'It was as much me as it was you. But I don't think it's a good idea.'

'No, of course not. I feel the same. Can we just forget this?'

Ouch. Surely him agreeing with what she had already said shouldn't hurt quite so much?

It was just her ego, she told herself. And her ego had no business sticking its nose into this. All her decisions when it came to Rufus were to be made entirely by her head. No other body parts got a say in the matter at all. She had to be sensible about this because if the electricity in that kiss was anything to go by, this would get very dangerous very quickly if she wasn't on guard against it.

'It's already forgotten,' she said, and hoped he couldn't sense the size of her lie, because she was sure that she'd never told a bigger one.

They walked slowly back to the house, trying to ignore the atmosphere, but once they were enclosed in the porch it seemed to swell and fill the space.

Jess breathed a sigh of relief as the old iron latch on the door gave way, and they walked through to the space of the great hall. The fire was roaring now, the heating on full blast too, and Jess shed layers as she crossed over to the kitchen to put the kettle on, warming her hands on the Aga and waiting for the feeling to come back to her fingers. While the coffee was brewing she went digging around in the pantry, looking for mince pies. Lara knew that Christmas wasn't Christmas without them. They were the only saving grace of this time of year as far as she was concerned, and her best friend wouldn't have forgotten them.

'Looking for something?' Rufus asked, making her jump, and nearly topple off the crate she was using as a makeshift step stool.

'Mince pies,' she said, still making a mental inventory of what was on the shelves, sure that she must just be missing them somewhere. 'I know Lara wouldn't have forgotten.'

'Ah. She didn't.' He stepped into the pantry and squeezed behind her. She pressed herself against the shelf, trying to stop his body brushing against hers, but the sudden movement set her off balance again, and she fell back against him, just for long enough for his hands to rest on her hips to steady her.

'Sorry,' he said, snatching back his hands as soon as she had regained her balance. 'I should have realised there wasn't enough room.'

'Easily done.'

Jess tried to brush off the feel of his body against hers, but found that she couldn't do it quite so easily. She stepped back into the doorway of the pantry while Rufus scanned the shelves, until he pulled down a jar with a triumphant hurrah.

'Mincemeat,' Jess said, eyeing it dubiously. 'Don't tell me I'm expected to DIY them.'

Rufus scoffed. 'Oh, come on. Everyone can make a mince pie.'

'Not me.' She shook her head, but Rufus looked at her with patent disbelief.

'But you're a scientist!'

She laughed. 'You seem to have a very poor understanding of what a scientist does. I can confirm that at no point in my academic career have I been called on to bake.'

'Then I guess I'm going to have to teach you.'

'I'm unteachable. Many have tried.'

He smirked. Smug. 'Did they have a Michelin star?'

Jess rolled her eyes. 'Always with the trump card. Come on, then, do your worst. It'll make good content, if nothing else,' she added, trying to remember that when it came down to it, theirs was a business relationship.

But Rufus stiffened at the word 'content' and she knew she'd said the wrong thing.

'I just meant…'

'It's fine. I know what you meant.'

There was no point trying to backtrack, not when she could see how tense his shoulders were. How set his expression. She'd have to show him, not tell him, that she understood that his childhood home was more than just a pretty backdrop.

'Okay, what else do we need?' she asked. If they were going to bake she was at least going to pretend to be enthusiastic. 'Even I can guess that flour is on the list.'

They grabbed ingredients as he reeled off a pastry recipe and carried them all to the marble section of the worktop. To keep the pastry cool—she had the theory of baking down. It was the practical that she'd always failed.

She concentrated on rubbing butter into flour, aware of Rufus vaguely watching her from the side. When she had the breadcrumb texture she knew she was meant to be looking for, she turned to ask Rufus if it was done, but he opened his mouth to speak at the same time.

'I'm sorry for snapping.'

'It's fine. I understand why you did. I know how you feel about this place.'

'But I shouldn't have taken it out on you. That looks good,' he added, nodding at her mixing bowl. 'You can add the egg, and it might need some cold water but go steady. You don't want it sticky.'

Jess followed his instructions with a hefty dose of scepticism. She'd lost count of the number of times that Lara had tried to override her genetic inability to bake and had been left aghast at their joint failure. But Rufus was turning out perfect circles of pastry lids to cover the neat spoonfuls of mincemeat filling, and then cutting delicate holly leaves to decorate the tops. Really, he was too much.

She stood back for a moment and watched him work, absorbed in placing tiny holly leaves on the top of each pie, positioning them with an exactitude she saved for her lab work, before looking over the whole batch and tweaking a leaf here and there.

'I think…' she started, not sure how she was going to square this skill with what she knew of Rufus. All this…and he could bake. 'I think they're remarkable.'

Rufus laughed and Jess felt the tension

leach from her shoulders as the last of the atmosphere dissolved.

'I think you're easily impressed.'

She looked at her own batch of pies—which were, despite her best efforts, rather raggedy-looking—and shook her head.

'Baking is magic, not science. And I definitely don't have the touch.'

'Yours are very…charming.'

She laughed at the obvious exaggeration. 'That's generous.'

Still, Rufus slid both trays into the hot oven of the Aga and set a timer. Jess sipped at her forgotten cup of coffee and leaned back against the countertop.

'Do you need to go back outside?'

'That depends. Can I trust you with the pies?'

'Well, you set the timer. So if they burn I'm placing the blame firmly at your door. But I'll take them out when the buzzer goes off if that's what you're asking.'

'Okay, well, I'll just be out the back door. Shout if you need me.'

'I promise not to burn the kitchen down in the next ten minutes.'

He smiled and paused in the doorway, holding her gaze for a beat, and then another.

And the whole time she was aware that the longer they were trapped here, the stronger this connection between them seemed to be.

'Go,' she said, her voice not much more than a whisper. She needed him to walk away. From her. From whatever this was between them. Because she wasn't sure that she was capable of doing it all on her own. And she needed to, because the alternative was risking pain, and she'd had enough of that.

The timer pinged on the Aga and she grabbed a tea towel to pull the trays from the oven. She marvelled anew at the precision and beauty of Rufus's mince pies, and tried not to think about the fact that he'd just spent the last hour making them for her, just because she'd told him that she couldn't bear the idea of Christmas without them.

And that was a level of thoughtfulness and generosity that she could do without. Especially coming from someone she was already finding inconveniently attractive. She was just trying to remember whether she was meant to turn them out onto the cooling racks when Rufus clattered through the door with a flurry of snowflakes and a huge basket of logs. She rushed to help him, and they lowered the basket between them.

'I had it,' Rufus said, a slight frown creasing his forehead.

'It was nothing.' Jess replied, wondering what she'd done to annoy him now. Well, at least when he was scowling he was considerably less attractive. And she would take any help that she could get on that score.

'I'm going to grab another basket,' Rufus announced.

'Do you need any—?'

'I've got it under control.'

Okay, so he was clearly peeved about something. With any luck, he'd hold that thought for the next few days, until she could get away from him. Safely away from temptation.

Rufus leaned his forehead against the door of the woodshed. He shouldn't have snapped at her. It wasn't fair to take it out on Jess. It wasn't her fault that he was feeling this way. This desperate desire that was becoming harder and harder to ignore was entirely on him. Of course, she might be feeling it too. He wasn't completely oblivious. But he was the one who had to keep his feelings in check. He was the one who had sworn that he wasn't going to have a relationship, because relationships led to family—and he knew he couldn't be trusted with one of those.

But it wouldn't have to be a relationship, said a rebellious part of his brain. It wouldn't have to lead to anything. It was just the two of them. In the place he loved most in the world, with huge amounts of decadent food, opulent decorations and luxury booze. They could just walk away. They could have this time here and then forget about one another afterwards.

Except Jess didn't want a fling. Oh, he was pretty sure that she wanted *him*. But their aborted kiss and the way that she had jumped away from him in the pantry told him all he needed to know. She was fighting this too, and he was sure that she had her reasons. Who was he to disagree with her? He'd overstepped once by kissing her—what had he been thinking?

He wouldn't do it again. She was his guest, however strange the circumstances, and he couldn't have her uncomfortable here. He wanted her safe and warm, and happy. And that meant denying these impulses. And all he had to do was take himself out into the sub-zero temperatures every hour or so to counteract the fire that she had been stoking in him for the past twenty-four hours.

He concentrated on filling the basket full of logs. If the power went then they'd lose the storage heating and they really needed to keep at least a couple of rooms warm. He needed to make sure there were candles and a torch in every room too, before night fell. There wasn't much he could do about the weather, but he would make them as safe as he could if the worst happened.

He pushed the door to the kitchen with his shoulder and deposited the basket of logs next to the fire, and caught Jess draping a tea towel over something. When she looked across at him, his heart stopped for a moment. She was trying hard to hide it, but she was upset. As he stood back up, her lower lip slid between her teeth and she bit down, and then he knew something was badly wrong.

'What is it?' he asked, crossing over to her in three long strides and brushing her hair back from her face to see it better. 'Jess, did something happen? Is it your parents? Or Lara?'

'No, no.' She tried to fake a laugh, but it came out as a strangled gulp. 'It's nothing like that. I was just trying to turn out the mince pies and…well…'

She removed the tea towel to reveal a pile of sorry-looking pastry and mincemeat. 'I knocked the corner of the cooking rack, and… Gravity took care of the rest.'

He let out his first full breath since he'd walked into the kitchen and pulled her into his chest, his heart pounding with relief. He let his eyes close for a second while he regained control of his heart rate. And realised he had her head still pressed to his chest. He released her with a start and took a step backwards for both of their sakes.

'I'm so sorry,' Jess said, looking over at the demolished mince pies.

'It's just pastry,' he said. 'I saw your face and thought something dreadful had happened.'

'But they were so perfect.'

'It doesn't matter. Honestly. Did any survive the fall?'

She pushed forward a plate with two of her mince pies on it. Raggedy pastry and leaky filling and all.

'One each,' Rufus declared with a rush of positivity. 'I'll make us another pot of tea and we can eat these by the fire. What's the matter?' he asked as she stood locked by the countertop, her face still a picture of distress.

'I don't know. It's just… Christmas. And being here. And thinking about Mum and Dad at home without me. It's such an unhappy time for them. And I've just left them to it.'

'You said yourself you would be there if you could be,' Rufus said gently. 'You can't blame yourself for the weather.'

'But they're so unhappy,' Jess went on. 'Mum's so miserable, and so is Dad, and I don't know why they are torturing themselves. No, that's not true. I do know why. It's because of me. They stay together for my sake, and it's made things unbearable for all of us.'

Rufus cupped a hand around her elbow, pulling her gently over to a chair. 'Jess, did something else happen while I was outside?'

'Yes. No. Just a call from my mum asking if there was any change in the weather. The roads down there are clearing. She thought I might get back at the last minute. And the sound of her voice when I said it didn't look likely… I just don't know why they would want to live like that. It's hard enough seeing it from the outside. I can't imagine what it must feel like from the inside.'

Rufus resisted the urge to pull her close again.

'I'm sorry that she upset you,' he murmured. 'I wish there was something I could do.'

She let out a long breath, her body relaxing a fraction.

'There's nothing you can do. Nothing I can do either. Believe me, I've tried. They've made their decision. They're both old enough to know they could make a different one.'

Rufus sighed. 'It doesn't make it any easier for you. To see them so unhappy.'

She shook her head.

'No. No, it doesn't.'

'Is this why…?' he started, but then stopped himself. He was massively overreaching. Whatever her reason for walking away from the kiss that they had barely started earlier, for jumping when his body had brushed hers by accident, he was sure that they were good ones. And none of his business.

'Why what?' she asked, looking up at him and meeting his gaze. And, with her eyes locked on his, caution was impossible.

'Why you're wary of this. Us. This…spark.'

She stiffened, leaned away from him. But it wasn't anger on her face. It was something closer to fear.

'I never said that.'

'I know. I'm reading between the lines. Woman who grows up seeing her parents in an unhappy marriage is wary of relationships.'

'We're not having a relationship.'

'I know that. And I have my own reasons for being wary too. But if you're steering clear because you think all marriages end like your parents', I just want you to know that you're wrong.'

'Well, thanks for mansplaining that to me. I'm aware that not every marriage is unhappy. My point, Rufus, is that any marriage can *become* unhappy. In the space of a day. A moment. Relationships are tested all the time, and some of them fail. Misery can blindside you. Just like that.'

He crossed his arms. Stared at her.

'I just think that's sad. That you'll deny yourself because you're scared of the worst.'

'I walk away from one kiss. Tell you one snippet about my life and you think you know me. You don't know the first thing about me.'

Well, that was a challenge if ever he heard one.

'I know something,' he said, maintaining their eye contact. He held it—another challenge—but she dropped her eyes and looked away.

'Look, I'm sorry about the mince pies,' she said, getting up and making a pot of tea, bustling and never meeting his gaze. She poured them both a cup, grabbed the plate of mince pies and headed for the door to the great hall.

He walked through a few moments later, finding Jess on the sofa closest to the fire, her legs curled under her and her hands clasped around her mug. He came and sat opposite her, and took the mince pie from the plate that she nudged towards him.

'I'm sorry,' they both said at once, and he smiled, saw the expression reflected on Jess's face.

'Can we start again?' he asked. 'Your mince pies are delicious.'

She laughed. 'That sounds like a very dodgy euphemism.'

'I'm offended. I never joke about mince pies.'

She snorted, contemplating the thick, uneven pastry. 'It was really kind of you to help me bake.'

'I enjoyed it,' he said honestly.

'Oh, my goodness,' Jess exclaimed suddenly, 'the pictures! We didn't get a single one before I dropped them.' She rolled her eyes and groaned.

'It's fine. We can make more tomorrow. What did you want to do with the rest of the day? I'll find something for lunch soon.'

'How about I beat you at a couple of games of Scrabble in between reading and Christmas movies?'

'That sounds like a challenge.'

'Oh, it absolutely is.'

She was scrupulously well-behaved while they played, even passing up the chance of a triple word score on an absolutely filthy word that she knew would make Rufus blush. Because they were being scrupulously well-behaved. They were resisting the temptation that had led them to nearly kissing earlier, because it was the sensible thing to do.

And that was why she was packing herself off to bed at little after nine in the evening when she didn't have work, or anything at all, to do the next day. Because her self-control could only stretch so far, and Rufus was testing the limits with every passing minute.

CHAPTER FIVE

WAS JESS AVOIDING him or had she slept in? This house was big, but not *that* big, and he'd know if she'd left her room. But it was nearly ten and there had been no sign of her since she had retreated to her room ridiculously early last night. That had to be on purpose.

Thank goodness she was being responsible and showing a level of self-control that he wasn't sure that he would be able to match if the tables were turned. Because everything in him was telling him to go and seek her out. Not to *do* anything, but just to hang out. He was probably just lonely. The electricity was out again, which meant no Wi-Fi and no connection to the outside world. She was literally the only person he could talk to.

And he knew that that fact had absolutely nothing to do with why he wanted to see her. He just *wanted* to.

Eventually, just when he thought he might actually lose his mind, she wandered into the kitchen as he was making a coffee, pulling a tray of mince pies from the Aga.

'Hey,' he said, trying to keep his voice neutral. 'Remind me not to leave you alone with these.'

'Oh, hi,' Jess said, faltering in the doorway, a trace of a smile on her face. 'You made more mince pies.'

'You said it wasn't Christmas without them.'

They stood without saying another word while the kettle boiled to a whistle.

'Coffee?' Rufus managed to say. And then, 'What are your plans for today?' As if he were a regular person who could string a sentence together in front of the woman that he fancied, rather than a tongue-tied teenager.

Jess faked a weak laugh, and he stopped what he was doing to narrow his eyes at her. 'What?' he asked.

'So... I just spoke to Lara and she had this idea. I think it's ridiculous, but she's pretty adamant.'

Rufus crossed his arms and leaned back against the worktop. 'Why do I feel like I should be worried? Very worried.'

'She said that you had a licence to use this place as a wedding venue.'

He felt blood rushing to his cheeks, and tried to hide the flush with a cough. 'Yeah, it's a big money-maker for venues like this.'

'She wants some pictures to appeal to that market. She wants me to make a veil out of a lace tablecloth or fashion a flower crown out of mistletoe or something. She just told me to make sure it looked romantic. Tell me you think she's being ridiculous.'

'She's being ridiculous,' he said, but there was a catch in his voice.

'But?'

'But…' He hesitated. Was he really going to say this? 'It is an important revenue stream. And when I was in the attic, I *may* have noticed that my mother's wedding dress is boxed-up up there.'

'You're kidding me.'

'I sort of wish I was.' He groaned. As if his feelings for Jess right now weren't complicated and inconvenient enough, they had to start talking weddings? But Lara was right. The wedding industry was a big market. He couldn't afford to ignore it—or to ignore Lara's advice. However much he might suspect that she might be meddling.

'Your parents must have got married in the eighties, right?' Jess said, and he guessed she was looking for an out. 'I bet your mum had big poufy lace dress. It's not going to work for Instagram.'

He shook his head. 'Actually she wore a replica of my great-grandmother's dress. Edwardian. Kind of beautiful.'

Her eyes lit up. 'Then she's not going to want me to play dress-up in it.'

'Why not? Pretty sure it was in the fancy dress box when we were kids. She's not precious about that sort of thing.'

'You're really going to make me do this?' she asked, her eyes wide.

'I'm not going to make you do anything, Jess. I hope you know that.'

'You're as ridiculous as she is,' she retorted.

He shrugged. 'Lara's your best friend. You must like ridiculous sometimes.'

Jess rolled her eyes. 'I can't believe I'm agreeing to this.'

Rufus smiled, just a little. 'You're agreeing?'

'Ugh.'

Jess contorted her spine, but it was no use. The dress had two dozen buttons up the back and there was no way she could reach even half of them. She looked in the mirror and tried to decide whether she was decent enough to call Rufus in for his help. She'd done the buttons at the base of her spine—the dress fitted perfectly—but there was still a swathe of bare skin up her back. And she wasn't going to get any more covered up without help.

The dress was cut high at the front, with lace sleeves. Once these bloody buttons were fastened she would barely have an inch of skin on show. But for that to happen…she was going to have to invite Rufus in here. And then she was going to have to stand while he slipped button after silk-covered button through the tiny loops that traced a path up her spine. Would have to stand there and pretend that the thought of his fingers so close to her skin wasn't making her burn up with wanting him. Making her second-guess all the very good reasons why she had pulled away from that kiss the day before, and told him—and herself—that it wasn't going to happen.

'Rufus,' she called, crossing to the bedroom door and opening it a crack. 'I think I'm going to need some help here.'

She turned back from the mirror when she heard the creak of the door and Rufus stopped dead on the threshold, his lips slightly parted, his mess of red-brown curls falling over his forehead.

'You look…'

She blushed as she waited for him to finish that sentence, but, wherever it had been going, he seemed to have fallen permanently off track.

'I can't get the buttons,' she explained, turning so that he could see the back of the dress. 'Do you think you could…?'

He cleared his throat and she looked away. It was too much, trying to maintain eye contact when he was looking at her with such naked appreciation. Desire. Need. Her eyes clashed with his again in the pitted reflection of the cheval mirror and she let her lids close, avoiding what was impossible to ignore.

His fingers brushed against her skin as he slipped each button through a loop, and she finally let out a breath when he reached the nape of her neck, tumbling her hair over her shoulder to keep it out of the way.

She stared at her reflection. Was this… real? She'd told herself for so long that she would never want this. That marriage was a trap—that at some point, when you least expected it, it would become a source of misery. And yet, looking at herself wearing this dress, with Rufus standing just behind her, watching her, she could imagine wanting it. She wanted him. She understood for the first time how people could take that risk. Because some things couldn't be ignored or avoided. Not for ever. Sometimes you had to take a risk, because walking away was impossible.

She heard the click of a shutter and knew that Rufus had taken a photo of her, still looking wide-eyed in the mirror. He moved to change the angle, and she turned to look at him over her shoulder, wishing she could know what he was thinking. Whether the sight of her in a wedding dress had freaked him out as much as it had her. He looked intent, focused on the screen of his phone, and she wasn't sure whether the twin lines between his brows were concentration or something else. One of them was going to have to do something to break this tension before it broke her.

'Where should we do this?' she asked, and Rufus glanced up at her with surprise.

'What did Lara suggest?'

'The only thing she said was to stay away from cliché.'

'So let's do something different.'

'Like what?'

He smiled, and she melted a little, before pulling herself together. 'Let's go to the kitchen.'

Rufus walked ahead of her—the narrow skirt of the dress hampered her slightly on the stairs—and when she reached the kitchen Rufus was shaking icing sugar over the cooled mince pies and arranging holly leaves on a plate.

'I thought we were taking pictures?'

'We are. Come. Sit.'

He pulled out a chair at the table, and she noticed that he'd moved some decorations around, so that there would be boughs of greenery behind her in the shot.

He placed the plate of mince pies in front of her and she raised an eyebrow in question.

'You're meant to look like it's your wedding day. Which means you have to look like you're in love.'

'Which means mince pies?'

'I saw the look on your face when you ate the last one. It was something to behold.'

'You're laughing at me.'

'Trust me, I'm not. I'm very happy to have put that look on your face, by any means. Now, are you going to eat the pies?'

'It feels…exhibitionist, doing it with you watching. Knowing you're taking pictures.'

He held her gaze for a beat.

'In a good way?'

Heat rushed to her cheeks and she decided there was nothing that she could possibly say that wouldn't inflame the situation further, so she closed her eyes, resigned, and bit into a mince pie. She could feel the powdered sugar on her top lip, and the filling was still warm. There was a hint of something spiced in the pastry and as her eyes closed she heard the click of the shutter again. She flicked a glance up to Rufus, and caught him grinning, looking down at the phone screen.

'Perfect,' he said, and she felt a little strange, knowing that he was looking at her face on the screen as he spoke. 'Next stop, the great hall.' She narrowed her eyes at the amusement on his face but followed him anyway. He pulled a stool out in front of the Christmas tree and she watched as he grabbed an umbrella from the stand by the door and climbed up on the stool to remove the star from the top of the tree.

'How do you feel about climbing up here?' he asked, pulling a bench further away from the tree, and then looking down at the screen, kneeling down and playing with different angles.

'What did you have in mind?'

'I thought if you stand up here, and jump, and we get the angle right, it'll look like you've got the star on the top of the tree.'

She grinned. 'What could go wrong?'

'Want to try?'

She nodded, reaching to take the star from him, and taking his outstretched hand as she struggled to climb onto the bench with her lace skirt.

She frowned at Rufus, down on one knee with the phone. 'Am I close?' she asked, holding the star in what she thought was about the right place. Rufus dipped lower, until the phone was resting on the floor.

'I just can't get it. Can you jump?'

'Jump? In this?'

'I can't get the angle right. If you can't jump, I could lift you?'

'Someone needs to take the picture.'

'We can prop it up on something. Use the timer.'

'You've completely lost the plot.'

'Possibly. Do you trust me enough to give it a shot?'

She rolled her eyes. This was going to end in tears. She was sure of it. But she threw her hands up. 'Okay, if you think it will work. My life in your hands and all that.'

He set the timer on the phone and ran the three paces over to the bench. His hands were on her waist before the red light started flashing and she barely had a chance to catch her breath before he had lifted her straight in the air. She reached out to clutch his shoulders, squealing with the surprise of it, and as the flash popped she realised she hadn't even tried to get the star in the right place.

Rufus showed her the result on the phone and she couldn't help but laugh—her arms were flailing, her eyes were wide and her mouth wide open in a shocked grimace.

'I think we may need another attempt,' she said, looking up and meeting Rufus's eyes.

The second and third attempts weren't much better, and on the fourth Rufus's arms began to shake as he held her as high as he could. She managed to remember to reach the star into the spot that made the angles work, and the results were definitely improving.

'One more?' Rufus asked, scrolling through the results.

She nodded. 'One more. Might as well turn on burst mode so that we've got the best chance.'

Rufus fiddled with the settings and propped the phone back on the floor. She waited on the stool while Rufus ran over to her, climbing up beside her and then hoisting her in the air with a very unflattering grunt. She reached the star as best she could, and tried to remember to do something balletic with her legs so she didn't look as if she was launching herself at Rufus in a rage. The burst of shutter sounds stopped, and she dropped her hands to Rufus's shoulders to steady herself as he lowered her.

She was pressed flush against Rufus as he let her down beside him, his hands burning through the lace at the waist of her dress. 'Do you think we got it?' she asked, her hands still resting on his shoulders.

He blinked, and she wondered whether he had heard her. The way he was staring at her right now, he definitely looked as if he had other things on his mind. Her gaze dropped to his mouth just as his tongue darted out and flicked over his lower lip. She pulled her-

self away, remembering the talk she'd given them both yesterday. The one where she'd reminded herself of why she didn't want to do this. Rufus's arms tightened around her waist for just a fraction of a second before he let her go.

They filled another couple of hours with laughter and slightly dubious photography—Rufus found her sheepskin boots and a huge checked blanket, and dared her to take some pictures outside. She posed in the wedding dress with their snowmen, threw snowballs at the camera, and felt her cheeks and her nose redden with the cold, until she had to admit defeat and retreat to the fire.

'This afternoon I was thinking fire, blanket, book,' she said carefully. 'Want to join me?'

Under a blanket? Any day. Except he couldn't say that out loud. He shouldn't even be saying it in his head. He needed to be more careful than that. Couldn't slip into the flirting that seemed to come so easily to them when they weren't fighting it hard enough.

'I agree that sounds like the best kind of Christmas Eve plan. But there are some things I need to do first. How about we watch a movie in a bit?'

'Sure.' Jess shrugged. 'But what's so pressing on Christmas Eve? It's not like we can even leave the house.'

'I know. But the weather forecast is predicting more snow tonight. A lot of snow. I just want to make sure we're prepared.'

She narrowed her eyes. 'If you say so. Though I doubt much has changed since the last time you checked.'

That wasn't the point. At this moment, they were both dependent on him to ensure that they were safe and secure, and he couldn't just sit back and hope that nothing would go wrong.

'There are just a few more things I need to deal with. I'll be back soon. Promise.'

Jess's phone buzzed in her pocket as she watched Rufus walk away.

Oh, my God. Oh. My. God. What is going on with you guys?

Jess sighed. If only she knew she might be able to tell Lara.

Don't know what you're talking about. It's just for the Gram.

Then she took a few atmospheric shots of her cosy set-up in front of the fire and hoped that would satisfy her friend.

Cosy. But the followers want more of Rufus!

Followed by a whole line of aubergine emojis. Subtle.

Well, Jess knew how the followers felt. There were parts of her anatomy that wanted a whole lot more of Rufus too. It was a shame that following those desires would be such a terrible idea. Not least because their recent conversation had made it perfectly clear that he wanted her too.

Not only that, but he'd also seen exactly why she was holding back and made her question herself.

She knew that her reasons for not having a serious relationship held up to scrutiny. There was no way that she was opening herself up to the chronic misery that had been eating away at the family for a decade.

But they weren't necessarily talking marriage here. In fact, it was hard to imagine a scenario less likely to lead to a serious relationship than two strangers with nothing in common being holed up in a remote lo-

cation before one of them returned to their home hundreds of miles away. Well, if her home was hundreds of miles away. In all the drama of Rufus's arrival, she'd half forgotten the job offer she'd received at the conference. But she'd promised to let them know her decision in the new year. She should be at least thinking about what she wanted to do for the next few years.

But even if she was living in the same county, she was hardly committing to him. No, what they had here were the perfect ingredients for a no-strings-attached fling.

She couldn't understand what was making her hold back. Rufus had told her already that he had his own reasons for not wanting to get involved—but did they extend to something casual? Something they could walk away from before the new year, and pretend had never happened? That was a very tempting thought. She snuggled deeper into the cushions on the sofa and let her eyes close as a series of very tempting scenarios for how they could spend the afternoon crossed her mind.

Rufus could find her here, in front of the fire, pull the blankets around them as they slipped down onto the rug in front of the hearth.

Or he could lift her in his arms, carry her up the stairs and across the gallery to deposit her on the giant bed that dominated her bedroom. He'd pick her up as if she weighed nothing and throw her on the bed, holding nothing back.

Her eyes flew open at the creak of a floorboard behind her, and she felt her cheeks flame because there was only one person it could be.

'Sorry, did I wake you?'

She answered *no* automatically, without thinking, and now she had to come up with a reason she was lying here with her eyes closed and her face burning red.

'Resting,' she told him lamely. Like an elderly aunt or a pre-schooler.

'Resting,' Rufus said with a smirk that made her wonder whether he had guessed the real answer—*I was just lying here fantasising about you carrying me up to bed with your big, manly arms.*

It was bad enough that she was thinking things like *big, manly arms* without him being able to guess how lame she was.

But from the look on his face, he didn't exactly seem to mind that.

'Did you sort out…whatever it was you

needed to sort?' she asked, cursing the way that words deserted her when too much space in her brain was being occupied by inappropriate fantasies.

'Nearly done. I want to double-check the batteries in the torches in the upstairs rooms.'

'Do you really think that we'll lose power again?'

He shrugged. 'I don't like how the lights keep flickering. If the storm tonight is worse than yesterday then I wouldn't be surprised. Either way, I want us to be ready.'

'Ready for action,' Jess said, and wanted to face-palm herself. Why did her mouth do this around him? Why couldn't she put sensible words in the right order, just because she was preoccupied with how much she liked his arms, and his beard, and his thighs? And the fact that he heard more than she said out loud.

'I just want to protect you,' Rufus said with a catch in his throat that Jess wasn't expecting. She leaned forward, resting her elbows on her knees. Well, this conversation just took a swerve, she thought.

'Why does that sound like we're talking about more than the blizzard?'

'We're not,' Rufus said, shaking his head. 'You're a guest here. I'm responsible for you.'

Right, and that was all there to it…

'You've been responsible for a lot of people the past couple of years,' she said.

'What's that meant to mean?'

'It's not meant to mean anything. I just find it interesting that after a time taking on big family responsibilities now you're all anxious about protecting me when I never asked you to, never expected you to, and really don't need you to.'

He frowned. 'Fine. Then I'm doing it for myself, if you don't need my help.'

'It wasn't a personal insult, Rufus.'

'This has nothing to do with my family's circumstances,' he barked, angry.

'Fine. Forget I said anything.'

She wasn't sure how the conversation had descended into this. She'd obviously hit a nerve, but that didn't excuse Rufus turning into a bear about it.

'I'm sorry,' he said, dropping onto the other sofa. So much for her fantasies about blankets and fires and…well. She'd try not to think about too many of the details.

'The thought of the weather and how the house is going to stand up to it is putting me on edge. I shouldn't take it out on you. And I never wanted to imply that you need taking care of. Or that it should be my responsibility to do it.'

'Apology accepted,' Jess said, deciding not to prod any harder at the sore spot she'd identified. It was none of her business if he had hang-ups over what had happened with his family over the last couple of years. If he felt guilt about moving them out of Upton Manor. After the snow melted and Christmas was over, she'd never see him again. He could nurse his wounds—or ignore them—however he wanted, and she'd never think about it. Or him.

'Did you get much reading done?' he asked, and she seized gratefully the change of subject and atmosphere.

'About three sleepy pages,' she replied, sitting back on the sofa. Reading at a snail's pace with no footnotes. No pressure. Bliss.

'Are you still up for a movie? Now that the power is back?'

'Sure. If it means I don't have to leave this spot for the rest of the afternoon. Except maybe to get snacks.'

'Or dinner,' Rufus suggested.

'Right. Dinner. My body clock is so far off when I'm not working. Do you know what Lara had planned? She's the real foodie.

I don't in any way pull my weight in the kitchen.'

'Come explore with me,' he said, standing and holding out his hand.

She raised hers, trying not to advertise the fact that she was having to brace herself for the idea of his skin on hers. It would be so much easier if she were immune to this. If she could just be indifferent. But if there was a key somewhere for turning these feelings off, she didn't have a damn clue where to start looking for it.

Her fingers met his and her hand slid into his palm as she tried to hide a wince of pleasure at the contact. Surely it shouldn't be so sudden, so immediate, so automatic—her response to him. He'd only touched her in a way he might help an elderly relative, and it had made her dizzy for him.

She wondered whether he felt it too. Whether the way he flexed his hand when he let go of hers was just easing some ache or pain, or if he had felt the same pulse of energy that she had.

She followed Rufus through to the kitchen and lingered by the door of the pantry while he scanned the shelves, aware of the heat that she had felt when they had shared that tight space the day before. But she had jumped away from him then out of instinct, because she hadn't wanted to find herself on a slippery slope that would inevitably lead to feelings and heartbreak. But she'd had time to think since then. To think, specifically, about what she wanted. Because the *who* was clear. She wanted Rufus. And she was starting to think that if she wanted, if they both wanted, they could lay down some hard boundaries about keeping this temporary and just take what they were both clearly craving.

Now all she had to do was find out if that was what Rufus wanted too. She wouldn't normally be hesitant in asking for what she wanted—but she wasn't normally in the position of having to live alongside the person who turned her down if that was the way this was going to go. She wasn't going to force a conversation that would make this situation more difficult. If it happened, it happened.

She realised her eyes had dropped to Rufus's arse just at the moment that he turned around and caught her. The corner of his mouth quirked up and she wondered if he was going to call her out on it.

'You thirsty?' he asked, brandishing a bottle of prosecco. She raised an eyebrow. Boy, was she.

'In the fridge for later?' she suggested, and she wondered whether Rufus was being deliberately provocative, because she was well and truly provoked. But she wasn't going to bite, or drink, yet. Not until she could be sure that they both knew what they wanted and were going to be able to extract themselves afterwards pain-free.

They gathered crackers, cheese, chutney and antipasti and created a luxury picnic spread on the coffee table by the fire. Jess tucked her legs under her and piled her plate high while Rufus looked through the Christmas movies on the streaming service.

'What do you reckon,' he asked as she spooned chutney onto her plate. 'Rom com? Action? Sentimental?'

'Action. Definitely action,' Jess replied. They were stirring up plenty of atmosphere without adding fictional romance to the mix. They settled on an eighties classic and Jess crossed the room to pull the heavy curtains, where the low winter sun was flooding the room with light and reflecting off the tv screen.

'It's really coming down out there now.'

Rufus came to stand behind her, reaching past her shoulder to pull the curtain back a little. The sky was heavy and dark, and the footprints they had made earlier were rapidly disappearing under a layer of fresh snow.

There was a draught coming from around the old leaded windowpanes, but Rufus's body was throwing out heat behind her. He smelled faintly of the fire and spices. All her Christmas fantasies rolled into one man.

She breathed in a big lungful of him, and couldn't help the smile on her face, just from knowing he was close. She could lean back, just a fraction, and she would be touching him. She could soak in that heat, feel her body relax into him. All as long as she could promise herself that she was going to be able to walk away afterwards.

She'd never had that problem before. But then, she'd never felt so drawn to someone either. The practicalities were going to take care of that. There were hundreds of miles between their lives. For now, at least. They had no reason to see one another again. It was two or three days. Four at most, surely. How hard could she fall for him in four days?

It had been forty-eight hours, and she'd managed to resist touching him, mostly. If things carried on moving at that pace... She wouldn't have done half the things she wanted to by the time she left. No, if she was going to act out even a quarter of the fantasies she'd been nursing since she'd clapped eyes on him, she was going to have to start asking for the things she wanted. Rufus had told her that he had his own reasons for not wanting to get too close. But if he wanted a fling, they could make this work.

One way to find out.

She turned her head to tell him exactly what she was thinking, and there was his mouth. She didn't want to talk any more. She glanced up and found his eyes on her, and then her eyes were on his mouth again, watching it move closer, until her eyelids fell closed and she gasped as she finally felt the brush of his lips against hers, just for a fraction of a second before he pulled away. She leaned in this time, reaching up on tiptoe to reach him, brushing their lips together a second time, feeling the curve of his mouth as he smiled. His fingers brushed against her jaw on their way to her hair, and she let his palm take the weight of her head. His other hand came up to thread into her hair, and she abandoned all control to him, feeling her face relax into a smile as his fingers wound through her hair and tilted her head. Taking his time to give her exactly what she wanted. When his mouth found hers again, it was hungrier, more demanding, and she opened her mouth to him, tasting him and taking what she wanted. Her neck and her toes were burning from trying to compensate for the difference in their height, and, just as she was starting to think that something was going to have to give, Rufus's hands left her hair and wrapped around her waist, lifting and turning her and pinning her to him so the whole of the front of her body was plastered against him. And he was every bit as hard and as soft and as hot as she had been imagining.

The cool draught from the window behind her raised hairs on the back of her neck, and all the time she was burning to be closer to him.

Her fingers eased between their bodies, seeking out the buttons in the soft flannel of his shirt, and she let out a growl of disappointment when she eventually found her way underneath and discovered more cotton rather than the bare skin she was desperate for.

Rufus broke the kiss, resting his forehead against hers, and all she could hear was the rapid gasps of their breath and the pounding of her blood in her ears.

'I've been wanting to do that since the minute you dragged me in here the other day.'

She laughed quietly. 'You were barely conscious.'

'And I still wanted to kiss you. I must have it bad,' he murmured.

She stiffened slightly. She'd got distracted and forgotten that she was meant to be doing this with boundaries in place. She probably should have got that out of the way before anyone started talking about having anything.

She tried to step away, before remembering that her toes had left the ground some time ago. She looked behind her, reaching for the windowsill, and Rufus let go as she hitched herself onto the cold tile.

'We should maybe talk about what that was,' she said, hoping that this wasn't going to throw too much cold water over the situation. 'And what it wasn't.'

Rufus ran a hand through his hair. 'Yeah. Well. I suppose we should.'

'You already know I don't do relationships. But if you wanted to do this, whatever this is, while we're here, then I'd like that. But nothing more.'

'I said I had it bad. Not that I was going to propose. You don't need to freak out.'

'I'm not freaking out. I just don't think it's fair to do this without us both having our cards on the table.'

'Good. I've seen your cards. Can we get back to doing what we were doing before we started talking about them?'

She grinned. If this was 'the talk' over and done with and they could get back to 'the kissing', then she was very okay with that.

She wrapped her legs around his hips in response and let out a squeak as he lifted her from the windowsill and carried her over to the sofa. He dropped back onto the seat so she fell in his lap, knees straddling his hips. She could just lean in and take everything that she had been fantasising about for the last two days. But she wasn't going to. Not yet. Not now she was allowed to just *look*. She'd been sneaking glances and trying not to let him see how she felt for too long, and the freedom to look at him without hiding how thirsty she was for him was almost as good as kissing him. At the very least, it was a delicious appetiser.

'You're not kissing me,' Rufus said, raising his eyebrows a fraction as his hands moved lazily from her butt along her thighs, leaving a path of heat in their wake. 'Why?'

She shrugged. 'I like looking at you.'

'I like you looking at me.' She lifted a hand to his chest, undid another button or two, and slipped her hands inside. 'I like you touching me.'

'Good. I was planning on doing it some more.'

Her hands explored lower, reaching for the hem of his T-shirt and pulling until she encountered warm skin.

'Don't stop,' Rufus gasped and she leaned in and dropped a kiss on his lips, and Jess moaned as his hands found her arse again. She'd meant to give him a playful peck before getting back to the looking. But she was drawn in by the heat of it, and couldn't drag herself away.

Rufus's hands went higher, to her waist, his fingers tightening and pulling her closer, until she wanted to climb inside his skin.

'God, it's amazing kissing you,' Rufus said, pausing to draw breath. 'You taste of mince pies. Like Christmas. I want to unwrap you.'

She laughed at the cheesy line, but she was with him on the sentiment. She lifted her arms above her head and welcomed the touch of cooler air on the band of skin exposed around her midriff. He grabbed the three layers of sweaters and lifted them over her head, leaving her in the silky slip that she had put closest to her skin that morning. Under the thermal layer that Rufus had found so funny yesterday.

Not so funny now that it was the only thing between her and the slight chill in the air that the fire hadn't banished.

Rufus's fingertips trailed down her arms, skimming the goose bumps, and then left her breathless as he flipped her back on the sofa, covering her with his body and pulling a blanket over the pair of them, creating a cocoon of warmth around them, a bubble of heat inside the old, isolated house.

She froze for a second at the sudden change of pace, and Rufus drew back, looking at her carefully.

'Is this okay?' Rufus asked.

'I…uh…' It was a struggle to form a coherent thought, never mind string words together, and the truth was, she wasn't sure what she wanted right now. Rufus sat up though, putting a little space between them. 'Maybe we need a breather,' he said. 'Christmas Eve is meant to be all about anticipation, and if we're not careful we're going to have torn through all our gifts before we even make it to Christmas Day.'

'Anticipation,' Jess said, pleased that Rufus had read the situation, read *her* so well. 'Got it. Good idea.'

Rufus felt as though he'd barely breathed for the past day, anticipating these moments when he was close enough to breathe Jess in, and now he was tearing himself away for the promise of more anticipation.

But really he needed to get his head together. They'd talked about what this was—or what it wasn't, as Jess had been so keen to specify. But she obviously still had her reservations, and there was no way that he was steamrolling them into something that she might regret. He didn't want to rush this. He wanted to savour it. Savour her.

'Where are you going?' Jess asked, propping herself up on her elbows to watch him as he drew the curtains and chucked a couple of logs on the fire before he sat down and pulled Jess into his lap.

'We said a breather; I didn't know you meant you were going to leave,' Jess murmured, turning her head and pressing a kiss to his throat.

CHAPTER SIX

'YOU CAN'T SEND THAT,' Rufus said with a grunt, looking at the photo on his phone screen.

'Why not?'

'Because you can see what I'm thinking.'

'Really? What were you thinking?' But she was only asking to tease him. He looked hot. Heated. He was looking at her as if he was counting the minutes until he could peel away her layers of soft, cosy knitwear to get to what was underneath.

It was undoubtedly a very good look on him.

And one that she wanted to keep for herself.

Just for the next few days.

After that she would give him back to the universe and have no claim on that particular expression. Jess pinged the photo to her own phone, and then deleted it, trying not to think too hard about the stab of regret she felt at the thought that soon—way too soon—she would be giving up the right to make him feel that way.

But she didn't have to do it yet.

She put the phone down, curled her hands into the front of Rufus's sweater and pulled him down for a kiss. And before she closed her eyes, she got another glimpse of it. That look that said he was going to burn her alive and make her thank him for it. She would. She would thank him and repay the favour and then he'd look at her like that again, and the house would become a black hole, pulling the emotion out of her. Making her spill more and more of herself.

She couldn't allow that to happen.

This was just a kiss. It might—she hoped, desperately—lead to *just* sex.

That was just bodies and skin and mouths. It was good and then it was over, and she wouldn't have to think. She never regretted what she walked away from because she knew the alternative to walking. The alternative was staying, the way her mum stayed. The way her dad stayed. And then you held those positions until you were empty. Until you'd given up on and forgotten the idea that life could be anything but that.

And she wouldn't do that to herself.

Walking had always been easy before. But she'd never had to walk away from Rufus. If she'd met him out in the real world—the one with passable roads and mobile phone coverage, she would have seen the danger right off. She would never have allowed herself the luxury of kissing him. But this wasn't the real world. This was a snowbound winter fairy tale that she'd be driving away from just as soon as the tyres on her rental car could handle the Yorkshire snow, and their paths would never cross again.

She would kiss him goodbye, and delete his number, and block him on Instagram and forget everything that happened here. She glanced at the photo again. But she wasn't sure how she was ever meant to forget that someone had once looked at her like that.

But that was the only plan she had, so she was going to have to go with it.

Her phone rang as she was looking at the screen, and she broke away from Rufus with a start.

'I… We… It's Lara,' she said, looking at the screen. 'She's video calling.'

She answered the call, too flustered to think about what else she should do, as Rufus ducked away from her so she wasn't left with trying to explain to Lara why they were sitting far closer than was reasonable for two people who hadn't just had their tongues in each other's mouths.

'Hey, Jess. What're you up to?' Lara asked. 'I loved the snowy pictures. Why did you stop? Did something happen to distract you there in your isolated manor with no outside interference? I can't imagine what that might be.'

Jess felt colour rising to her cheeks and wished she had the ability to hide her feelings from Lara. But her best friend had known her too long and too well to risk it.

'I knew it!' Lara cried, and Jess glanced behind her to make sure that Rufus was out of earshot.

'I don't know what you think you know, Lara, but you're wrong. There's nothing going on here.'

'Right. I don't believe you for a second. Just try and fit some more photography in around your extracurriculars, will you? I'm sending you a list of shots that I need. Get them to me as soon as possible. We are building some momentum here and it's killing me that I'm not there to do this myself. Whatever it is that you're not telling me, you can get back to it when I've got my content.'

Jess tried to hide a smile, not wanting to give away any more than she already had.

'One,' she said, rolling her eyes at the phone, 'I'm not up to anything. Two, we sent you photos this morning. Photos I froze my fingers off and got snow in my hair for. Three, stop being a drama queen. Send me the list and we'll get to work. Because there's nothing else I'd rather be doing right now.'

'Good. Send them over as soon as you can. And if you get into anything really extracurricular then be sure to keep those to yourselves. I'm not sure that either I or my followers could cope with that.'

'Get your mind out of the gutter, Lara,' she said with an affectionate smile. 'I'm hanging up now. Goodbye.'

'I take it we've got more work to do,' Rufus said, coming up behind her, wrapping his arms around her waist as soon as the coast was clear.

'Apparently we've been slacking. She wants more content. Lots more.'

'Sounded as though she might have wanted to know what we've been up to instead.'

'I wouldn't know what to tell her. We kissed. We agreed to walk away when we leave here. It's hardly the fairy-tale stuff her imagination is probably cooking up. Look, this is private, and I want to keep it that way. I don't want this thing to become something that generates clicks, you know. I want to keep it just between us.'

He turned her round in his arms, brushed his lips against hers.

'Which is why I'm so glad we're the only people here right now.' She let herself sink into the kiss, drowning in the heat and the size of him as he wrapped his arms around her shoulders, until his warmth and weight and bulk were all around her. Until her phone buzzed in her pocket, a message from Lara, no doubt, reminding her that she was on to her, expecting her to drop her extracurriculars—as she put it—and concentrate on content. She dragged herself away from Rufus, immediately missing the warmth of him.

'Me too. Really. But Lara is not going to leave this alone, so we had better get it over with.'

She pulled her phone out of her pocket and

scanned down the list. There were requests for various flatlays. Fine, she knew what she was doing with those: they were an Instagram staple. She just needed some props, a pretty surface to lay them on, good lighting and a steady hand to take a shot directly from above. But the full Christmas dinner would have to wait until tomorrow.

'Looks like we're going to be busy,' Rufus said, reading over her shoulder.

'This isn't exactly what I had planned for the rest of the day,' she said, in a snit. That eyebrow rose higher.

'You had plans? I want to hear them.'

She smiled as she raised her eyes to meet his. 'Who said they involved you?'

He let out a sound that could only be described as a growl as he dragged her back close, knocking her phone to the ground.

'They better had. Otherwise I'll start making plans of my own.'

She smiled as his lips met hers. 'Fine. I'm sure I can make room for you, if you insist.'

'Oh, I absolutely insist.'

It was only as she felt her body relax into his that she remembered that last time she'd been this close to him they had been interrupted and if they didn't get on with taking these bloody pictures then Lara would be interrupting them again. If there was one thing that she was sure about her plans it was that there was no space for Lara in them anywhere.

'We need to get through this list. I know Lara, and she will start cracking the whip if we don't get on with it.'

'Fine, I'm sure you're right,' he said, releasing her and reaching for where his phone had dropped to the floor.

'Well, we can't do the food today,' he said. 'The turkey will take four or five hours in the oven. But we can crack through the flat-lays.'

Jess scrolled through the list again, which had grown since the last time she looked. She was sure that Lara was trolling her, because since they'd last spoken there seemed to be a lot more call for pictures that involved her on a bed, with rumpled-up blankets, cable-knit socks and a tray of props beside her. And she knew that Lara knew it was impossible to get these kinds of shots without help. Lara had once drowned an iPhone in a full cup of coffee trying to get the perfect bird's-eye shot by sticking her phone to the ceiling. No, Lara knew that this would mean recruiting Rufus to photograph her lounging in bed, and if that wasn't such a deliciously enticing thought then she would definitely have been mad at Lara for meddling.

'Pictures in bed?' Rufus asked, raising an eyebrow. Her cheeks heated again, wondering if she and Rufus were having matching fantasies.

'Not like that,' Jess said, tapping the Instagram icon and pulling up a few pics from Lara's feed to show him what she meant. Rufus scrolled through, looking thoughtful.

'This is what she wants?'

'As close as we can get it.'

'Do I hang from the ceiling to get that angle?'

She thought of the afternoon she had spent in Lara's flat clambering on the bed frame, grabbing hold of ceiling lights, trying to get the perfect angle and lighting while keeping her feet and her shadow out of the frame.

That first time they'd ended up collapsing in a giggling heap in the middle of the bed once the iPhone-meets-coffee-cup disaster had been cleared up.

'There is generally climbing, yes.'

'And you're okay with this? Pictures of you in bed?'

She shrugged. 'There's nothing sexy about

it. The more layers of knitwear the better, as far as Lara's Instagram is concerned. She's usually up to her ears in cables and cashmere.'

'Then I guess we should make a start. What do we need?'

Jess reeled off a list of things they would need from the kitchen, from a tray of tea and snacks to a roll of foil for a reflector. Thankfully the snow outside was bouncing around plenty of natural light, so they shouldn't need too much editing. She was gathering blankets and cushions, considering colours and textures, when she heard footsteps behind her and Rufus shouldered open the door.

'This looks intense,' he said, taking in the piles of textiles she had gathered up as she walked through the house. He left the tray on the sideboard and came to stand beside her. 'This one lived on my bed,' he said, pulling a soft quilt from the pile.

'You didn't want to take it with you when you moved out?'

'It wouldn't look right in my flat. It's always been here. It would be weird to see it in a new place.'

She realised she hadn't actually considered where Rufus lived now. He was so much a part of the house, the house was so much a part of him, that she couldn't imagine him anywhere else.

'Where do you live?' she asked, and the surprise on his face made her wonder whether he'd forgotten too. Whether he was as caught up in this fantasy as she was.

'Oh, I share a flat in Upton with my brother. The village. I need to be close to the manor house for maintenance stuff.'

'I can't imagine you living anywhere but here.'

He shrugged. 'I moved out years before Mum and Dad had to leave. I was so focused on my career. I'd set myself a goal, and sacrificed everything trying to achieve it. I never expected to spend my whole life here but...'

'But you expected to come back. One day.'

'One day. Yes. I thought I'd spend my dotage here. And so did my dad. I guess we're both coming to terms with that.'

'Does it help if I tell you again that none of this is your fault?'

'I'm not sure how that can be true, when I was the one who abandoned this place. Abandoned my dad to deal with it all himself. But I appreciate the sentiment. How about you distract me instead?'

She felt her lips curve into a wry smile, aware that Rufus was quite deliberately changing the subject. But there was no point pushing him to talk if he wasn't ready.

'And how would you like me to distract you?' she asked.

He looked her up and down. 'First, by masterminding these photos so your phone goes quiet.'

Right on cue, it buzzed with another message notification and she knew Lara was still sending through her instructions.

'And then I'm going to trust your imagination.'

Good. Because her imagination was proving to be exceptionally vivid today, and she was looking forward to putting some of her ideas into action. All the more so now that she knew Rufus was along for the ride and wasn't going to ask more of her than she had to give.

She layered up blankets on the bed, and then dug through her bag looking for the knee-high socks she knew that she'd packed. She snagged them from the bottom of the holdall and pulled them on over her leggings.

She knew what this really needed was a plaid shirt, which she didn't have with her. But Rufus did. But it was a little early in this…whatever this was…to start wearing his clothes. Or undressing in front of him, come to that. She looked down at the soft fake cashmere she'd pulled on that morning. The colours and textures worked with what she had on the bed. It'd do for now. But if she found herself wearing Rufus's shirt at some point over the next few days… It wouldn't be the worst thing that could happen.

'Where do you need me?' Rufus asked as she pulled her socks up to her knees. Well, wasn't that the question…

'Um, on the bedside table? Are you okay to stand on it?'

'On the four-hundred-year-old antique? Sure.'

'Oh, God.'

'It's fine,' Rufus said, chuckling. 'It's survived four centuries. I think it can handle Instagram.'

'Right.' This had better be worth it. 'On that side of the bed though,' she said, gesturing over to the side near the window. 'We want the natural light behind you.'

'You're good at this.'

She lifted her shoulders and lct them drop. 'When Lara started out it was mainly the two of us messing around, making things up as we went along.'

'And you weren't tempted to follow her into being an influencer?'

She shook her head. 'I like my research. My job. I help Lara out because she's my friend and I love her, but I wouldn't want to do it all the time.'

She climbed into the middle of the bed, poured tea into the cup that Rufus had put on the tray with its saucer, and tried to arrange her limbs in a way that would get maximum knitwear into the shot and hide as much of her face as possible, all without spilling the tea. She'd seen Lara do this dozens of times, but had never tried contorting herself into these positions before.

'How's it looking?' she asked Rufus, who had one foot on the corner of the bed, and one on the bedside table.

'You look beautiful,' he said, checking his phone. She felt the blood rise in her cheeks at his compliment.

'This is meant to be about the house,' she reminded him.

'Yeah, that's holding its own too,' he said, snapping a couple more pictures.

Jess smiled to herself, deciding not to push

any further. The sexual chemistry was crackling as tangibly as the logs in the fire on the other side of the room, providing a hum of tension in her belly. A warm glow full of promise for later.

Rufus leaned a little closer, bringing the camera right overhead, and she turned slightly, letting her hair fall in a curtain to block her from view. She'd been on Lara's feed before, but wasn't wild about becoming the face of Upton Manor. That was totally Rufus's job. So if she could duck behind her hair, she absolutely would. Except Rufus seemed determined to capture her features. He leaned in closer still, causing the tray to wobble, and she looked up in alarm.

The click of the phone sounded just as her eyes reached the lens of the camera, and Rufus hastily backed up onto the bedside table and then dropped to the floor.

'Wow,' he said, looking at the screen. And Jess had to admit, she could see why he'd said it. He'd captured her as her eyes had widened when the tray wobbled. The doe-eyed result was pretty arresting, even if she said so herself. Rufus scrolled back so she could see some of the other shots and they had done Lara proud. The room looked beautiful, and she was happy that she'd managed to get all her limbs in the right place to set it off.

Rufus pulled up Lara's social media feeds and swiped through some of the shots that Jess had highlighted for him earlier.

'You know…' he said, looking closely at the photos '…if I were playing spot the difference here…' he pointed the phone in Jess's direction '… Lara seems to have socks on bare legs. Whereas you're layered up. If we were going for total @*lara* authenticity here, we need to match.'

'Are you offering to strip off for the camera?' Jess asked.

'I was offering to help you out of those leggings,' he said with a smirk. 'Just for artistic purposes, of course.'

Jess laughed, a little nervously. 'You're an absolute scoundrel. We're meant to be working.'

'A scoundrel?' Rufus's crow's feet crinkled as he smiled. 'Has anyone been a scoundrel in the last century? I've never been accused of being a bad 'un before.'

'Maybe Upton Manor is getting to me,' Jess said, leaning back on her elbows. She had no intention of sending Lara pictures of her wearing long socks with bare thighs. But that didn't mean that they couldn't have a little fun with the set-up they had here. It would be a shame to waste the opportunity to lose some clothes for a perfectly unimpeachable reason.

'Okay,' she said, letting just one corner of her mouth rise in a hint of a smile. 'Chuck a couple more logs on the fire, though. It's starting to feel cool in here.'

Rufus's eyes widened in surprise before his face broke into a grin as he walked to the fire and built it up. Good, Jess thought. He was planning on settling in for a while. She had an enormous bed, the most picturesque, romantic setting she could imagine, a gorgeous man doing her bidding, and she had every intention of pretending that this was real life for as long as she could get away with it.

She moved the props off the bed, and then crawled back among the nest of blankets, leaning back on her elbows as Rufus tended the fire.

He turned to her with a wolfish grin, before climbing up onto the foot of the bed, and pulling her towards him by the ankle. She laughed as he crawled towards her with intent, until his hands were planted either side of her head, his knees astride her hips. She turned her head and nipped at his wrist, smiling at his gasp of surprise and then squeaking when he pressed a kiss to her lips. And just as she was about to pull him down and deepen the kiss, he was gone, sitting astride her hips and smiling down at her.

'You bite,' he said.

She propped herself back on her elbows, closing her eyes for a second in pleasure at the weight of him on top of her.

'Sometimes. When I'm pinned…'

'I should let you go, then,' he said, but she grabbed the front of his sweater before he could move.

'Don't you dare.' She pulled him down for another kiss, firm but still sweet. And didn't object in the slightest when his hands smoothed down her thighs, across the sensitive spot behind her knees, towards the tops of her socks.

He pulled away, rolled on his side and propped his head on his hand, as he pulled her knee up. His fingers dipped into the top of her sock, teasing again at the back of her knee. Jess lifted herself up on her elbows again, watching. Her eyes locked on Rufus's fingers as they continued their exploration, slowly easing down her sock, until the skin of her ankle was exposed. She gasped as his fingers brushed against bare flesh for the first time. He looked up and met her eyes, his face consumed by a smug, masculine smile. She rolled her eyes, leaned forward and kissed him, before nudging him with her knee. The other sock came off considerably more quickly, and then she was lying beside him, his face intimately close as his fingers trailed along the waistband of her leggings. She bit down on her bottom lip, and watched his expression as he looked up. 'Okay?' he asked, nudging her sweater up, and she nodded enthusiastically as he hooked a finger under the elastic and started to inch them slowly down.

'Still okay?' he asked, and she pulled lightly at his sweater again, until she could reach to plant another kiss on his lips.

'Don't you dare stop.'

She sank back on the bed as the fabric passed her hips, and she had a brief moment to thank her morning self that she'd pulled on lace this morning. Had she known? Thought? Hoped? That this was where the day was headed? Of course she had. This was everything that she'd wanted when she'd woken that morning.

'So pretty under all these layers,' Rufus breathed, pressing a kiss between her belly button and the top of the lace. The soft hair of his beard tickled her, and she squirmed with pleasure. But then his mouth was gone.

Rufus watched, entranced, as inch after inch of soft, creamy thigh was revealed. He was certain he hadn't breathed in minutes. Maybe hours. And he couldn't now. Not when he was so close to Jess and fighting to keep his self-control.

He let out his breath as he finally slipped the fabric over her feet, and then skimmed his hands up smooth shins, past the point he'd found behind her knees and up to her waist.

It was only when he was sure that he had a handle on his self-control that he kissed her. And he only allowed himself a second before he pulled away. Getting naked hadn't been the plan here, and he had to remember that.

He reached for the socks, where they lay abandoned on the bed, and Jess looked up at him languorously as he knelt and pulled the sock over her toes, and then slid it up, letting his fingers lead the way, and drinking in Jess's gasps, the way that she let her eyes fall closed as she caught her bottom lip between her teeth and bit down.

'You're putting clothes back *on* me?' she

asked between breaths as he reached for her other foot.

'Of course,' he said, letting his face break into a smile. 'We need these photos, right? Otherwise we'd be downstairs drinking tea and watching a movie.'

'Right,' she said, her voice breathy and distant. 'Tea. Movie.'

Except when he pulled the sock up, and his fingers brushed higher, she arched her back off the bed, and he nearly lost his resolve.

She pulled him down to her by his sweater again, and it really was bloody brilliant when she did that. As far as he was concerned, she could grab him and kiss him every moment that they had here together. If it wasn't for one thing. He'd told her he was taking her clothes off for the sake of these photographs and he wasn't having her on. If she wanted to seduce him on her own time, on her own terms, he would let her do that. Once he'd done exactly what he'd promised to do, and not a thing more.

'Where are you going?' Jess demanded as he pulled himself away from her.

'This wasn't for me,' he said, gesturing to the milky white skin showing between her socks and her sweater. He picked up his phone and climbed back onto the bedside table.

'Are you…?' Jess turned to look at him. 'What are you doing up there? Get back here. I wasn't done with you.'

He smirked, took a photograph and showed her the screen. She looked divine in the warm afternoon light. Her lips pouted with dismay. Climbing back down, he regarded her all stretched out on the bed. She turned onto her side and regarded him carefully.

He smiled. 'It's Christmas Eve. It's all about anticipation. And,' he added softly, 'it's about making sure we both know what we want. And what we don't want. I was invited into your bedroom to act as photographer. If you want me for anything else, you're going to have to ask me for it. Specifically. Very specifically.'

'I hate you,' Jess breathed, dropping back on the bed and breaking their gaze, looking up at the canopy of the bed.

CHAPTER SEVEN

'No, YOU DON'T,' he told her confidently, leaning in to press the briefest of kisses to her lips. 'Now, let's get the rest of these pictures done for Lara. I want the whole evening with no chance of interruptions.'

'You do realise I'm going to have to put my clothes back on for that to happen.'

He groaned as she pulled on her leggings and layered up thermal socks. Anticipation might have made Christmas Eve magical when he was a kid, but it was downright killing him now. He watched Jess as she worked, taking a couple of pictures from different angles, dipping down until her eyes were level with the mattress. From there she got the twinkling lights and the crystal bowl from the sideboard in the background. And from a different angle, the window and the fire, the bright light darkening the foreground into moody silhouettes.

'I like that one,' Rufus said. 'The house looks lived-in. Cosy.'

He leant against the side of the bed as they scrolled through. Then she turned abruptly.

'Don't move,' she instructed. He rested his forearms on his knees while she adjusted something on the touch screen and then leaned back, pointing the camera in his direction.

'I like this one,' she said, showing him the result. 'It was missing heart. It needed you. You belong here.'

'Yes. Well. I used to.' He pushed himself to his feet. 'Let's get this finished.'

Two hours later, Jess scrolled through the pictures on the phone screen, trying to decide which to send to Lara. Not the ones of her on the bed, bare-thighed, her eyes full of lust. No, those were for her and Rufus only. But the others she could share. And her favourite: Rufus leaning back against the bed, arms propped up on his elbows. Lost in thought. Deliciously shaggable. Looking every inch as if he was as much a part of the house as the walls and the floorboards. No wonder he was mourning the loss of his family home. If only she could make him see that it wasn't his fault. But she knew it wasn't her job to do that. He just had to decide whether he wanted to hold on to that guilt or not.

She wondered whether that guilt had anything to do with those reasons he'd mentioned for not wanting a relationship. Not that it affected her either way. She'd been as clear with herself as she had been with Rufus that this was a strictly time-limited offer. Whether or not he was going to make something work with someone else once she was just a fond memory was none of her business. She had to make sure that she remembered that, otherwise she was going to find herself in trouble.

Rufus dropped beside her on the sofa and she leant into him without taking her eyes from the screen. It was just so…perfect…that he was there and she could do everything that she'd been wanting to do since he'd fallen so dramatically into this house and into her life.

Well, almost everything that she wanted to, until they'd put the brakes on things earlier. As if she wasn't at breaking point already. They'd studiously avoided touching each other while they'd taken the rest of the photos that Lara had requested.

She'd got Rufus in front of the camera as often as she could. He was the one who had wanted to show this house with personality, and heart, and he'd done just that. Had shown just how much he was a part of the structure of this house, and how it was a part of him. And the results were stunning, and bittersweet, because this wasn't Rufus's home any more, and might never be again.

But they'd done exactly what Lara had asked of them, and they had to hope that it would turn the business around, and that Upton Manor would at least stay in the family rather than having to be sold off. She highlighted the pictures that she wanted to send and synced them with Lara's cloud account.

'Are we done?' Rufus asked, pulling up the list and scrolling through.

'Everything but Christmas dinner. I've already told her that will have to wait until tomorrow, so I think we're officially off duty.'

'That is very good news,' Rufus said, his arm dropping to wind around her waist, and then dragging her onto his lap until she was as close to him as she'd been desperate to be for the past few hours. 'I've wanted this. You. All afternoon.'

'I thought Christmas Eve was all about anticipation,' Jess murmured.

Rufus groaned and glanced at the clock

above the mantel. 'It's hours until midnight. Well, at least let me feed you, because I'm pretty sure that you've completely missed the fact that it's dinner time. And then we could actually watch the movie that we said we were going to several hours ago.'

'And when you say we're going to watch the movie…'

'I'm open to distractions. When you're ready, if you're ready.'

His hands came up to cup her behind, pulling her down more firmly on top of him, tipping her forward until her forehead rested against his.

'But first, let's eat,' he said, pulling the blanket over her legs. And dropping a last kiss on her lips before he left through the door to the kitchen.

Thank God Jess's hesitation earlier had forced him to slow down. Because if they hadn't agreed to this breather, this chance to let the anticipation grow, he was pretty sure he would have lost his mind by now. But it was only a stay of execution; he didn't think for a minute that they were both going to keep a lid on their self-control for much longer.

And he didn't need to examine his feelings.

They had both agreed that they weren't letting feelings into whatever it was they were going to share while they were here.

He boiled some water for pasta. He'd stocked the freezer with a rich ragu sauce that would be perfect with tagliatelle and a grating of fresh parmesan.

Was he carb-loading them before a long night? All right, well, that wasn't the worst idea he'd ever had. He'd had a *lot* of ideas, and had no intention of getting any sleep.

Jess wandered through to the kitchen and leaned against the doorframe. 'That smells delicious. You were right. I absolutely need you to feed me.'

'See. You should trust me.'

'I do,' she said, her voice losing its playful tone. 'I trust you.'

He crossed the kitchen, throwing the tea towel he'd been using over his shoulder. Cupping both of her cheeks in his hands, he kissed her slowly, sinking them both against the doorframe.

'Good. I'd never hurt you.'

'I know.' She hesitated though, and he knew there was more to that sentence.

'But…' he prompted.

'No buts,' Jess said. 'These few days are

what they are. It's what we agreed. What we both want.'

'If you've changed your mind—' he started, before Jess interrupted.

'I haven't. Not about what I want. Not what about what I don't want. I'm not sure what's making me feel melancholy.'

'Christmas blues? Are you missing your family? I know you said Christmas is hard with your parents. But sometimes the hard thing is still better than the…alternative thing.'

She rested her forehead against his chest and he threaded one hand into her hair, pulling the other tight around her waist.

'I do miss them. It doesn't make sense to be sad about it.'

'What's sense got to do with anything?' he said into Jess's hair. 'If you're sad, you're sad. There's nothing wrong with that.'

She looked up at him from under her fringe.

'Thank you,' she said. 'You're sweet.'

'Hmm. Don't tell anyone.'

She grinned.

'Who would I tell?'

A timer went off behind them and Jess turned towards the noise. 'Tell me I can eat whatever it is that smells so amazing.'

He smiled. 'Why don't you pour some wine?' He gestured to where he'd left two glasses and a bottle on the table 'And I'll serve up.'

When he found her at the table, bringing two steaming bowls, Jess let out a moan of pleasure. Rufus was right. Being away from work and out of her usual routine was messing with her body—she was absolutely starving. Thank goodness Rufus was here to remind her to eat, because left to her own devices she wasn't sure that she would be able to think beyond her need to be close to him.

She only had a moment to thank fate that she had met him here. Now. Where they had strict boundaries in place, imposed by geography and the weather. Because if she'd met him at home, at a party, in a bar, she would have run a mile. She would have recognised their chemistry, how potent it was, and she would have known that she wouldn't be able to handle it. But here, she knew she didn't have to rely on her self-control to keep things simple. Circumstances would mean that she couldn't fall deeper into this than she could pull herself out. Circumstances made this safe. Made Rufus safe. Though when she thought about it, it wasn't Rufus she had to worry about. It was her own mind, her own heart, that she had to be careful of. But here they had a built-in escape route. She didn't have to keep her defence guarded, because this wasn't going to last more than a few days, whatever happened. Which meant that she could sink into tonight—whatever adventures it brought—with no reservations.

And she was going to positively *dive* into this pasta. Was Rufus so intent on feeding her up because he had big plans for her tonight? If so, she was totally on board with that. He should start mainlining carbs himself, because all this thinking time they were giving themselves was helping her come up with a long, detailed list of everything she wanted to do with him.

'This is incredible,' she said, taking her first mouthful of pasta. 'How did you knock this up so quickly?'

'It was in the freezer. I cheated. I told you that food's part of the deal. Sometimes I come in and do a supper club thing, sometimes I just stock the fridge and freezer, depending on what the guests want.'

'Well, I don't know which one of you I love more right this minute. Lara for asking you or you for cooking it.'

'I am fully prepared to take the credit,' Rufus said with a smile that seemed slightly strained. Was it because she'd said the L word? Surely he couldn't read too much into it when she'd dumped him into the same category as her best friend. It was the same sort of simple, platonic love that she'd feel for anyone who cooked her a meal this delicious. She decided to take a large sip of wine, and hope that the atmosphere eased without her having to address the issue head on.

They gradually eased back into small talk as the pasta in her bowl rapidly receded, and by the time she eventually laid down her spoon and fork he was back to giving her long, heated looks that made her want to start tearing off items of clothing. His. Hers. She didn't really care, as long as some garments started hitting the floor fast. He met her gaze and smiled.

'I know exactly what you're thinking,' Rufus said. She thought for a second of telling him he couldn't possibly read her mind. If it wasn't for the fact she knew that what she was thinking was written all over her face.

'And...so?' she prompted, hoping that his mind-reading abilities extended to giving her exactly what she wanted.

'Pudding first,' Rufus said, and, although she had been hoping to skip straight past it, if the dessert was anything like as decadent and rich and delicious as the main course, it would be worth putting their evening on hold for, just for a few more minutes. No longer, though. She was still hungry. And not a saint.

'Shall we take these through with us?' Rufus asked, pulling a couple of chocolate puddings from the Aga and turning them out into bowls. Thick chocolate sauce oozed from their centres and ran down the sides, settling in a pool of rich, melty goodness, so delicious-smelling that it was enough to wipe any disrobing plans she'd had clear from her brain. Well, for as long as it would take to devour that pudding.

She snagged the glasses and wine bottle from the table while Rufus brought the pudding, and then she burrowed into the blanket nest that they'd abandoned earlier. Rufus handed her the pudding and a spoon, and she couldn't even wait until he was sitting beside her before she took that first delicious mouthful.

She moaned with pleasure, and by the time she opened her eyes Rufus was sitting next to her with his eyes full of intent.

'I think I'm just going to eat this until midnight.'

'I'm not sure I'm that chuffed about being replaced by a pudding.'

'Well, you made the pudding. So it's not like you're *not* entertaining me.'

'And yet I can think of ways I'd rather be doing that.'

'*And yet…* Christmas Eve, anticipation, et cetera.'

He lifted his spoon to his mouth, and she watched, enraptured.

'You're right, though. If we're going to resist temptation, this is as good an alternative as I can think of.'

'Amen to that,' Jess said, loading up her spoon again.

She sank deeper into the sofa cushions as Rufus reached for the remote. 'Shall we hit play?'

'Mmm,' Jess agreed, her mouth still full of chocolate. Rufus laughed as he pressed play and the first notes of the opening credits rang out of the sound bar under the screen.

Jess's spoonfuls of pudding grew smaller and smaller, eking out the sensual pleasure contained in the bowl for as long as possible. And—she shot a sideways look at Rufus—

perhaps delaying the moment when they would both have their hands free.

The great hall was lit with just the sparkling lights from the tree and a few candles on the sideboard, one of which must be responsible for the delicious spiced winter berry scent that was currently diffusing around the room.

When her bowl was scraped clean, and her spoon licked of any trace of chocolate, she looked up and found Rufus watching her again. Amused.

'I was worried for the pattern on the bowl.'

'If it had tasted as good as the chocolate did, it wouldn't have survived.'

Rufus laughed. 'Great commitment,' he said. She decided to completely ignore the C word, as he had with the L word earlier. There was no reason it should freak her out, all out of context as it was.

Rufus pulled the bowl from her hands and put it on the coffee table along with his own.

'Come here,' he said, pulling her close and wrapping his arms around her waist from behind.

He wondered how long he would last before he broke and kissed her. He hadn't been exaggerating earlier when he'd told her how much he loved kissing her. It had hit him like a punch to the gut, that moment when her lips had met his and confirmed this attraction was entirely mutual and entirely explosive.

It had taken all his self-control to keep that kiss light. To invite rather than demand. And then when Jess had told him what she wanted, and it fitted entirely with what *he* wanted— walk away, no strings—he'd wondered if he'd dreamed her up.

His wrist brushed against bare skin as he wrapped his arms around her waist, and Rufus gritted his teeth as he demurely pulled down Jess's top and tucked the blanket around her shoulders. It was a good job pulling the curtains had left them almost in darkness, because he was sure that if he could see what he was feeling right now, the ping of his self-control snapping would be audible three counties over.

Glass shattered in a hail of bullets and Rufus reached for the TV remote to turn the volume down. He shifted round to get a better look at Jess's face, and nearly came undone at the sight of her teeth closing on her bottom lip.

His hand threaded into her hair, and he

soaked in the glorious tangle of it. His thumb reached to brush against her cheek and she smiled, shifting so that he was above her on the sofa, her body angled beneath him.

He held his breath as he leaned in to kiss her. 'You taste of chocolate and red wine. You are every delicious treat today.'

She smiled at him. 'Because you haven't let up feeding me.'

He leaned into another kiss. 'I like looking after you.'

'I wasn't complaining,' Jess said, reaching for him and pulling him back down.

The fire of bullets sounding on the TV made Jess jump and they both laughed as Rufus reached for the remote and turned the volume down even lower.

'So much for watching the movie,' Jess said, her hands coming to rest on Rufus's shoulders. He pushed her hair back from her face, dropping kisses where her forehead was exposed.

'I'd rather watch you,' he said, smiling.

'What happened to anticipation?'

'It's lost its shine. Is this okay? Midnight feels like it's days away. Weeks.'

Her hand reached round to the back of his neck, pulled him down for a deep kiss.

Rufus groaned at that, because no amount of waiting could make this feel more right. He couldn't imagine any way that it could feel more perfect than it did right now.

Until Jess shifted under him, revealing that band of bare skin at her waist again, and this time he couldn't—didn't have to—stop himself from dropping his hands there and exploring. 'Is this okay?' he asked as his fingers stroked the soft skin of her belly, and one of her legs coiled around his, locking their bodies together. He pulled away to get a better look at her, and her eyes were undone and her cheeks flushed, her lips parted as she tried to catch her breath. It was without doubt the sexiest thing he had ever seen.

But he could only look for a second before he needed to kiss her again. How had she done this to him? She had only been in his life for a handful of days, no doubt would be gone from it again soon—it was what they'd agreed. It was the only future that this had, but he felt a pang of regret, going into this knowing that it couldn't last. That was his choice, he reminded himself. More than a choice. It was an obligation. He'd decided not to have a relationship, a family, because he knew that he couldn't be trusted to put their needs above his own. Jess hadn't believed him when he'd told her it was his fault his parents had had to leave Upton. That it was the backdrop to luxury mini-breaks and Instagram photoshoots rather than the family home it had always been meant to be.

She'd been insistent that there was nothing else he could have done—that he wasn't to blame for going off and chasing his own ambitions rather than staying here and supporting his father. All of which was easy to say when she hadn't been there. Hadn't seen the disappointment in his dad's face when he'd learnt that even when he was released from hospital, he wouldn't really be going *home*.

'Rufus?' Jess pulled back, looking at him. 'Are you okay? Where did you go? You were all in your head.'

'I'm here,' he said. 'I'm here, with you.' He punctuated each word with a kiss. 'For however long we have.'

For however long we have.

Why had those words given her shivers? Maybe it was the words, or maybe it was the fact that Rufus's hands had resumed exploring under her sweater, inching higher as he pressed kisses to her lips, her jaw, her neck.

She reached down for the hem of her sweater and Rufus pulled his body away from hers, giving her room to work, though his lips didn't break from hers until she dragged the fabric in between them, revealing the silky vest she'd put on that morning, wondering—hoping—that this was where the past few days had been leading.

Rufus's breathing was heavy as she dropped her sweater on the floor, and his eyes were kind of dazed.

'Bed?' he asked, and the broken gravel of his voice would have been enough to get her there with him even if she hadn't spent the last three days going out of her mind with wanting him.

'Bed.'

CHAPTER EIGHT

'REMIND ME AGAIN why we waited three days to do that?' Rufus said, his eyelids as heavy as his limbs. Beside him, Jess was still trying to catch her breath, and he pulled her closer with an arm around her waist.

'Because we're idiots,' she said, turning towards him and pressing a kiss to his chest before settling her head on his shoulder. 'Just so you know, I'm not waiting three days for round two.'

She yawned; Rufus tensed. No, because in three days the snow would probably be gone, and so would she. But now was not the time to be thinking like that. Not when Jess was warm in his bed and there was still a foot of snow down the lane. There would be plenty of time to lament how little time they'd had once this was over.

Jess reached for the phone in her jeans

pocket, where they'd landed on the floor, and he turned to spoon her, pulling the blankets close against the cold air of the bedroom. 'It's past midnight,' she said, dropping the phone on the bedside table and turning in his arms. 'Merry Christmas.'

'Merry Christmas,' he murmured, kissing her again. 'This is absolutely the best start to a Christmas Day I've ever had.'

'I should hope so.'

Rufus woke in the morning to goose bumps on his shoulders where the blankets had been tugged down, and the tip of Jess's nose cold against his chest. He grabbed a couple of blankets from the floor and tucked one around Jess as he eased himself from under her arm, and then wrapped the other around himself while he went to tend to the fire. They had been too distracted to remember to build it up last night and were paying the price for it now.

He poked the last few embers and added some kindling, waiting for the flames to lick up the knots of newspaper before adding a few logs.

He looked towards the bed where Jess was still sleeping soundly, and smiled. He wished that he had known to wish for her before now.

He shivered in the chill of the room and pulled on more layers, knowing that the great hall would be positively arctic with the fires burned down low. He opened the door just a crack, not wanting to wake Jess, then decided to wrap the blanket back around himself as he went out into the cold.

'Nice cape,' Jess said, and Rufus turned towards her. She'd startled him, she realised, and wondered what had him so distracted that he hadn't heard her coming. She slipped her arms around his waist under the blanket and pressed her cheek into his chest, hoping that this wasn't about to get weird. With morning afters, there was generally at least the option of a hasty exit if one of the parties decided that they were having second thoughts. But neither she nor Rufus had an escape route— even if one were needed.

He turned to rest back against the Aga and opened the blanket far enough to wrap her up with him as he leaned down and brushed his lips against hers.

'Good morning,' he murmured against her mouth. 'I was going to bring you coffee.'

'Then I should have stayed in bed. I was

cold, though. Thought I'd see if I could find someone to warm me up.'

'How's that going?' he asked, his hand cupping her cheek as he turned her head to one side and trailed kisses along her jaw.

'I found this great big guy with a cape…' she said, eyes rolling as Rufus's lips found the spot on the side of her neck that made her utterly melt. 'I'm wondering if he's up for it.'

'He was planning on making you breakfast first, so you're going to have to decide what your priorities are.'

'Sex, food or coffee? You really want me to choose?'

'You've got about three more seconds of that,' he said, his voice cracking as her hand slipped into the waistband of his trousers, 'before coffee and breakfast are off the menu.'

She held up her hands, all innocent, as she took a step away.

'Feed me. Caffeinate me. Take me to bed. In that order,' she said, laughing. He shoved a plate of toast at her.

'Eat quickly.'

'Efficient. I like it,' she said, sliding onto the bench on one side of the big oak kitchen table, staying close to the heat of the Aga. 'Are we meant to be cooking already?' she asked, glancing at the big clock on the wall and trying to remember how long Rufus had said that the turkey would take to cook.

'It's already in the oven,' he said. 'It'll need hours, so we don't have to do anything yet.'

'Good,' Jess said, finishing her toast. 'Because I was planning a few more hours in bed. Are you coming?'

When Jess woke later that morning, the house smelled of Christmas. She wasn't sure whether it was the pine branches on the fire, the smell of roast turkey, or Rufus beside her that smelled the most delicious. Or maybe it was this exact combination. Perhaps if Rufus could bottle it and sell it, it would solve all his financial troubles.

She propped herself up on an elbow and looked down at Rufus, still fast asleep on the pillow next to her. How had she ended up here? Well, she knew how. And why. Because Rufus was officially scorching hot, and she had a lot less self-control than she'd thought she had. But how had she found herself with a guy that she really genuinely liked, and— it turned out—was incredibly compatible with, and really, really, didn't want to leave. This was the sort of situation she had spent her whole adult life avoiding. She could tell herself that she was just going to walk away when the snow cleared, but sooner or later she was going to have to face the fact that she felt…more…just *more* than she had for anyone else for a long time. And when they finally got out of here, maybe walking away wouldn't be as easy or as painless as she had convinced herself it would be before they'd slept together. Not that she had any regrets on that front. Some things were worth a little pain, and sex with Rufus definitely fell into that category.

'You know it's creepy to wake up and find someone watching you.'

She smiled as Rufus rubbed sleep from his eyes and then leaned in for a kiss. She had meant to keep it light, teasing, until Rufus's fingertips brushed the nape of her neck, holding her close to him, and her whole body sank into him, hot against his side from her shoulder to her toes.

'I have to go and baste the turkey,' Rufus said at last, breaking their kiss.

'That had better not be a euphemism,' Jess said, falling back on the pillow and watching as Rufus pulled trousers and what looked like half a dozen sweatshirts on. He laughed and leaned in for a last kiss.

'Nothing weird. Just your actual, literal, Christmas dinner to cook.'

'I must have been really, *really* good in a past life,' she mused, noting the smug smile that turned up the corner of Rufus's mouth.

Really, it was a good job that they weren't going to get a chance to get used to this, because he would be seriously hard to walk away from in the real world.

'I'll jump in the shower then come and help,' Jess said, dragging herself upright and wrapping one of the blankets around her shoulders.

'Thanks, but I think I'll have enough to do without you randomly throwing things on the floor.'

She threw a cushion at his head. 'One time! I dropped the mince pies one time.' She laughed as the cushion landed back on the bed beside her and Rufus blew her a kiss.

Half an hour later, she followed him into the kitchen—it had been nearly impossible to drag herself out of the scalding hot shower. The fire wasn't kicking out much heat yet, and when she checked the dial on the electric heaters they were already turned up as high as they would go.

She pulled on enough layers to keep the chill out, and then added a scarf for good measure.

'You look toasty,' Rufus said, grabbing her for a quick kiss before turning back to the pots steaming away on the stove.

'It's nice and warm in here,' she said, unwinding the scarf and pulling up a stool. 'Are you sure there's nothing I can do?'

'I'm sure,' he said, checking the potatoes quickly, and then coming to the table with a cup of coffee for them both.

'Merry Christmas,' he murmured, tucking her hair behind her ear and brushing a lingering kiss to her lips. She moaned, wondering if they couldn't just skip Christmas and spend the day in bed instead.

Except she had felt her phone buzz in her pocket twice already, and she guessed it would be Lara hassling her about the pictures they had promised her.

'I'll take the action shots, then,' she said as Rufus pulled out a knife and started chopping carrots. As she pressed the button on the camera, the lights flickered and for a second she wasn't sure if she had blinked and imagined it until she saw the expression on Rufus's face. It wasn't just her who'd seen it—he had too, and he was worried.

She slid her arms around him from behind and rested her face against his back. 'Don't worry,' she said. Not that she understood why he was so tense about the power going out. This house was more than four hundred years old. She was sure that they'd manage if they lost power for a while.

'It could be fun,' she said. 'A blackout, I mean. Candles. Fires. Just each other for entertainment…'

'No phones. No heating. No way of contacting the outside world in an emergency…'

'Presupposing an emergency happens, when we have no reason to.'

'Yes, well, emergencies don't tend to announce themselves in advance. They just sneak up on you and your life is suddenly changed and you don't know how it happened.'

She thought for a moment. 'Like your dad's heart attack.'

He directed a scowl in her direction. 'My dad's heart attack has nothing to do with this.'

She crossed her arms, not prepared to let him off the hook. 'If you say so. That traumatic event must have barely affected you at all. I don't know what I was thinking.'

Reaching past him, she stole a carrot stick, crunching as she watched him rearrange his features into something neutral.

'How about we don't worry about it until it actually happens? I know you've already prepared everything you could. I trust you.'

She saw the muscle of his jaw tick and pressed a kiss there, reaching as she did so for more of the carrots.

He tapped the back of her hand playfully, the atmosphere between them easing a little. 'If you keep eating them at this rate, there'll be none left for dinner.'

She huffed, taking just one more. 'What can I say? You wore me out. I need to refuel.' He smiled at that, and she let herself breathe a little easier. Things had threatened to get heavy there for a minute and that had never been what this was about. They had agreed that this was just a bit of fun. And there was nothing fun about digging into one another's hang-ups. She certainly wouldn't have wanted him digging into hers. It was just hard, seeing him so obviously hurting over something that had been so completely out of his control.

But it was Christmas, and she would avoid arguing if only for the sake of that.

'I'm not sure Lara's followers are interested in me peeling carrots,' he said, his features warming to her.

'You look hot with a speed-peeler,' she said, taking another couple of pictures.

'What, like this?' he asked, holding a particularly large carrot in a way that bordered on obscene, reducing Jess to a fit of laughter.

'I am definitely not sending these to Lara,' she said, showing him the photo reel. He laughed too, and suddenly she could breathe again. Until her phone started ringing, and her mum's name showed on the screen.

'I have to take this,' she said, moving a step away from him. She knew this was going to be hard, and having Rufus listen in would only make it harder.

She walked through the door to the great hall as she swiped 'Answer' on the screen.

'Hi, Mum,' she said. 'Happy Christmas.'

'Happy Christmas,' her mum said, obviously trying to inject some jollity into her voice, but Jess could hear how fake it was.

'Are you and Dad having a nice morning?'

'Oh, you know…'

And she did—she did know. And it broke her heart.

'Mum, do you think…?' She took a deep breath. Thought of all the hints that she'd dropped all those years, and all the times that she'd stopped short of coming out and saying what she'd been thinking. 'Are you happy?'

Her mum's silence said it all.

'Because I worry about you,' Jess went on. 'I really want you to be happy. Dad too. And I don't think you make each other happy any more. Not since we lost Charlotte. I'm sorry, but it's Christmas, and I just can't bear the thought that you two have been miserable all this time, and if what you think I'll feel if you split up is any part of why you haven't, just… don't. Please.'

'Jess, your dad and I love you very much.'

'I know! I know you do. But you don't seem to love each other any more. You don't seem to make each other happy. And maybe we should all go to lots of therapy together. I don't know. I just know that something should change. Because the way things feel isn't right.'

It had taken this—being here, away from her family—for her to realise that she couldn't just carry on. She couldn't get through another Christmas with all this unsaid. Something had to change.

She spoke to her mum for a few more minutes, assured her that everything was fine at Upton, and the local weather reports were expecting a thaw in a couple of days. She even managed a couple of words with her dad before the lump in her throat got too big to ignore and she made her excuses and hung up, with promises that they would all talk some more when she got home. She sat on the sheepskin in front of the fire, winding her scarf round her neck while she looked into the flames, wondering how her family had been reduced to this. Wondering whether she'd invented those childhood memories of laughing, happy parents, noisy Christmas mornings, ripping through paper with Charlotte.

No, she reminded herself. Those memories were real, and she owed it to Charlotte to remember that. To fight back against the pit of despair her parents threatened to pull her into. That they had pulled each other into. She just wished that she could make them happier. That she could undo the years that they had spent not talking about how they really felt and being miserable instead. The years that she had spent without her sister. With a part of herself missing.

It was the reminder that she needed, at just the right time, of why she didn't do this. Why she didn't get involved. Why she had agreed to walk away from Rufus when the snow was gone. She was never going to live how her parents did. And if that meant walking away from a man like Rufus then that was what she would have to do.

'Hey,' said a voice behind her, and she looked up to find Rufus leaning against the staircase, watching her. 'Are you okay?' he asked, crossing over to where she was sitting on the floor. He sat behind her, his strong thighs bracketing her hips as he pulled her back against him and wrapped his arms tight around her.

Jess nodded, not trusting herself to speak just yet, and Rufus pressed his lips to her hair.

'I'm sorry you're sad,' he said gently. 'Today especially. Is there anything I can do to help?'

'This,' Jess said softly. 'This is good. This is helping.'

She rested her head back on his shoulder and let her eyes fall closed. She *would* walk away from this when the snow was gone.

It was the only way to protect herself from repeating her parents' mistakes. But she was here now. And so was Rufus and they both knew what this was. So, she was going to soak this up, and absorb enough comfort from his body as he would give her.

'Mmm,' she murmured. 'Is that roast potatoes I can smell?'

'And here I thought it was my body making you feel better. You're only in this for the food.'

'In my defence,' she said, opening her eyes and turning her head so that she could see his face, 'the food is spectacularly good.'

He grinned. 'And the rest?'

'Satisfactory, so far,' she said with a smirk.

And then before she knew what was happening, she was on her back, the sheepskin rug tickling the back of her neck as Rufus loomed over her. She hooked her ankle around his as a shiver of anticipation shot through her body.

'Satisfactory,' he repeated, his face deadpan as he lowered to his elbows, pressing the breath from her chest—as if she even cared about breathing just now.

'Sounds like I need more practice,' he said, his lips brushing her temple, her ear, her jaw.

'You're going to burn the potatoes,' she said, biting her lip to stifle a moan. The only thing that felt better than what Rufus was doing right now was winding him up while he did it. But then his mouth was on hers and there were much better things to do with her tongue than talk.

'They're crunchy.'

'You say crunchy, I say burnt.'

'They're crunchy, and I don't regret a minute that they were in the oven.'

She smiled. 'Good. I should hope not.' She tipped the potatoes out into a serving dish, and snapped a few shots for Lara.

'Do you think we made enough?' she asked with an ironically raised eyebrow at the banquet laid out before them.

'So I don't know how to cook for two. It's fine. There's lots of space in the freezer. Are you done with that? Do you think we're going to get to eat any of it while it's still hot?'

'I'm nearly done,' she said, pouring gravy on the two full plates she'd staged with silverware and glasses on a table in front of the kitchen window, where they could take advantage of the natural light. And once the photo shoot was done, Rufus whipped a couple of hot plates from the Aga and carried them through to the dining room, which had been too dark for the camera, but was the perfect backdrop to an intimate dinner that they had barely wanted to dress for. Rufus had laid one place at the head of the table, and the other just to one side. The centrepiece had been pulled over between them, so that their little corner of the grand dining room was every bit as cosy as any table for two.

She slid into the seat beside Rufus and reached for the wine bottle, pouring them both a generous measure of the rich, delicious burgundy that they had opened the night before.

'Are you feeling better?' he asked as she tucked into the roast turkey.

'Yes, much better, thank you. I didn't expect to feel sad today. I thought I felt like that because I was forced to spend it with my parents.'

'But it turns out you were sad anyway.' He reached for her hand and squeezed. 'And that's okay. You miss your sister. The way your family used to be. The way your life used to be.'

'Yes. I think you're right. Just like you do,' she answered and waited for his automatic denial. But instead he frowned, a crease appearing between his brows.

'Yes. Like me, I suppose,' he said. 'We have that in common. Lives that could be simplified by the existence of a time machine.'

'I'm not sure that a time machine ever simplified anything. But I wish I could have Charlotte back. Failing that, I need to find a way to be happy without her. I can't go on hiding from the problems in my family for ever.' He squeezed her hand, and her heart swelled a little at the unspoken support, and had to remind herself that its presence was only temporary. She couldn't rely on him to make her Christmases bearable, because this time next year he would be long gone. No, she was going to have to figure that one out by herself.

She pulled her hand from him, shaking herself into the present. 'Come on,' she said, picking up her cutlery. It would be criminal to let this food go cold. They chatted as they ate, and she felt the sadness fade. The warmth and cheer that she and Rufus had found here gradually pushing out the darker parts of her heart, making room for something else. Someone else. He wasn't going to stay there. She knew that. They both knew that. But it made her wonder. When this was all over, was she going to let those parts of her creep back to how they had been before? Or was she going to keep pushing against those thoughts and feelings that made her unhappy and see if she could replace them with something new? It didn't have to be Rufus. She didn't want it to be a man. She'd seen what had happened to her parents when they had given too much of their hearts to another person for safe keeping and found them inadequate to the task. But she could fill it with *her*. She could look at the hurts that she had absorbed from her parents and decide whether she wanted those parts of her past making decisions for her.

Or she could embrace Christmas the way that she and Charlotte had when they were children and decide unequivocally for herself that joy in the Christmas season was going to be her gift to herself this year.

She smiled as she reached for one of the crackers on the table and held it out to Rufus.

'We're missing something,' she said, and Rufus narrowed his eyes at her.

'What's going on?'

'I want to see you in a stupid Christmas hat,' she said, shaking the cracker at him now.

'Give over. I wore your bobble hat for hours. Wasn't that enough?'

'Nope. You wore the hat because I was saving your life. This is to entertain me, and I find that I'm full of Christmas spirit. And that means you have to wear the paper hat.' He scowled at her and she pouted shamelessly. 'Unless you want to ruin Christmas completely.'

He groaned as he pulled the cracker, and the contents spilled onto the table between them. Jess picked out the hat from among the detritus and stood up, leaning to pull it onto Rufus's head. But then a pair of muscled arms was wrapping around her waist, pulling her into his lap.

She shrugged, trying to suppress a smile. 'Fair trade,' she said, pulling the hat further down onto his head, linking her hands behind his neck and leaning back to get a better look at him.

'Very festive.' She laughed at his frown and pulled her phone out of her pocket for a selfie. 'Are you pouting for the camera?' she asked.

'No. Just for you,' he said, finally breaking and cracking a smile. 'What's brought about this sudden burst of festive cheer?'

She shrugged, and couldn't help but notice that Rufus's eyes dipped to her cleavage as she did so. Good. Having his mind there fitted perfectly with her plans for the rest of the day.

'Oh, nothing,' she said, shrugging again, and very much enjoying the expression on Rufus's face when she did so.

'Just been thinking about a few things. Deciding a few things.'

His brows drew together for a moment.

'Good things?'

'Very good things,' she confirmed, pulling herself close again, until her nose bumped against his, and his eyes closed as a smile spread over his face. 'I've decided not to be sad at Christmas any more.'

'That sounds like a good decision,' Rufus said, his hands curving round her bottom and pulling her in tight. 'Let me know if there's anything in particular I can do to make you happy.'

She smiled, and brought her mouth to his.

'Oh, I've got an idea or two,' she said, between kisses.

'Well, Merry Christmas to me,' Rufus gasped.

CHAPTER NINE

JESS LISTENED TO the *drip-drip-drip*, wondering whether rain indoors was something that she should be sufficiently concerned about to pull Rufus's arm from around her waist, open the hangings on the four-poster bed and extract herself from the warmth of the quilts and of the man sleeping soundly beside her. But the constant sound of water was causing another problem—one less easy to ignore—and that cast the deciding vote. She would set all sort of speed records diving into the bathroom and be back in the bed before the sheets had cooled.

She inched out from beside Rufus, untangling their legs and pulling gently on her hair where it was caught beneath his head.

He moaned softly as she slipped from the sheets, but she pulled the bedclothes higher and watched as he drifted back into sleep.

Without her. She stood and looked at him for a moment, not able to put her finger on why that should cause such a sharp pang of regret. This wasn't the first bed that she'd slipped from before dawn. Not the first time she'd left someone sleeping, not even realising that she wasn't beside them any more. Rufus was dead to the world. It absolutely was not rational to be annoyed at him for something he had done—or not done—while he was sleeping. She grabbed a blanket from the foot of the bed and wrapped it around herself as she went through to the bathroom.

When she returned, Rufus still slept soundly. And there was still that drip-drip-drip that had made it so impossible for her to fall back to sleep.

Drip.

She spun, looking for the source of the sound.

Drip.

She spun again. That was it. There was no point getting back into bed until she'd found where it was coming from and reassured herself that the ceiling wasn't about to cave in on them both.

Drip.

It was coming from near the window. She

crossed to that side of the room, checking the floor for puddles and the ceiling for suspicious-looking damp patches, but couldn't see anything out of place.

Drip.

She drew back the curtains and watched as a single teardrop of water slid down an icicle hanging from the lintel outside, and hit the sill below.

Drip.

That was it. That was the sound that had woken her, that had made it so impossible to get back to sleep. It was the thaw. It was the snow and ice receding. It was her and Rufus…leaving. She settled on the windowsill, pulling the blanket tight around her, tucking herself in, right up to her neck as she leant against the side wall of the window seat and followed the slow but inevitable progress of each drop of ice melt from the icicle to the ledge below. She looked out over the driveway and the lane. It looked no different than it had yesterday, but she knew that was deceiving. The temperature had risen, probably by just a degree or two, and that tiny, barely perceptible change would be all it took to melt the intimacy that had grown between her and Rufus in the four days that they had been here.

She jumped as the curtain jerked back behind her, and she found Rufus, rubbing at his hair with the heel of one hand, the other finding the nape of her neck, absentmindedly winding into a curl there as he leaned towards the window pane, his breath misting the glass.

'It's thawing,' he said, his hand stilling on the back of her neck. 'The ice is melting. The snow soon too.'

She leant into his hand, rested the side of her head against him as he stood even closer. They watched the window, the icicle beyond it as the sky lightened. The sun crept over the horizon, sending streaks of pink and red and purple across the sky. Jess wasn't sure when Rufus had slipped onto the seat beside her, when his arms had sneaked around her waist and pulled her back against his chest. All she knew was that by the time the sun was fully up, her fingers and toes were ice, the dripping had stopped, and she never wanted to move.

'How long, do you think?' she asked at last.

'Until the road is clear?'

She nodded, suddenly finding it hard to speak.

'Tomorrow. The day after at the latest.'

'We should make the most of being here, then. Together…'

She tried to make her voice light. Playful. Tried to make it sound as if this was just what they'd said it would be all along. Just something fun. Something they would both walk away from without a backward glance when they left this place. Rufus kissed the top of her head. And now she was watching the snow melt, making no effort to move, and wondering what she had done. Why her heart hurt at the thought of this beautiful landscape looking lush and green in the spring.

'What do you want to do today?' Rufus asked, his voice a rough murmur in her ear. Involuntarily, her arms tightened around his, locking them together.

'This,' she said. 'Or drawing the curtains and pretending the sun isn't up yet.' She held her breath, not sure how Rufus would react to that. The first time she had so much as hinted that she wasn't going to be just walking away from this as if nothing had happened. He found her hand under the blanket and brought it to his lips.

'You're cold,' he said, his voice gruff as he stood, holding out a hand to pull her up. 'Let's eat,' he said, his face inscrutable. 'We'll make a plan when you're warm.'

Jess wrapped her hands around her mug and grinned as Rufus served her avocado and poached eggs on toast.

She could get used to this.

Or…not. She reined in her imagination, her smile faltering. There were a million places she could get avocado on toast. She didn't need Rufus for that. She didn't *need* him for anything. He was a nice added bonus to this delicious breakfast, that was all. She had to keep reminding herself of that.

'What does your Boxing Day usually like?' she asked.

'Mum and Dad used to force us outdoors and the habit's stuck. The last few years we've gone ice skating at the rink by the church.'

'That sounds amazing. I'd love to go skating. I don't suppose you have a convenient frozen lake kicking around the place somewhere?'

He frowned, and then grinned mischievously. 'No frozen lake. But leave it with me. I have an idea.'

She grinned, finding his enthusiasm infectious. If this was to be her last day here, then she wasn't going to spend it brooding. She was going to spend it counting the times she could bring a smile to his mouth and he to hers.

'I will actually explode if you keep feeding me like this,' she said, leaning back, leaving half a slice of toast on her plate.

'Well, I have an idea if you want to work it off,' he said, and she hit his arm affectionately.

'Get your mind out of the gutter.'

'Get *your* mind out of the gutter, lass,' he countered, smiling. 'That's not what I meant. Wait here. Don't leave the kitchen.'

'Oh. You in charge. I like it.'

He leaned down and kissed her on the lips. 'If you want me to keep my mind out of the gutter, you've got to stop saying things like that.'

But he dragged himself away, and she reached for the teapot in the middle of the table, topping up her mug and wondering what he was planning.

He returned with a grin on his face and his hands behind his back. 'Close your eyes.'

'No way. God knows what you'll do to me.'

'Close your eyes or you won't get your surprise.'

She narrowed her eyes. 'I'd better like this.' Then she let them fall closed, waiting with her breath held. She started when she felt his fingers touch her foot, but he stilled her.

'Trust me.'

And how could she not, after everything that they had shared here? And then her foot was being pushed into a stiff, unyielding boot. She snapped her eyes open and was faced with the sight of Rufus trying to wrestle her foot into a neon pink rollerblade. 'Oh…my… were these *yours*?'

'My sister's,' Rufus replied. 'Mine are right here.' He pointed behind him to where a pair of black skates with fluorescent green laces sat on the tiled floor.

'Please tell me you know how to use them,' she gasped, excited at the thought.

'I know what I'm doing,' he said, tightening the ratchet at her ankle and making her gasp. 'Do you?'

'Nope. Not in the slightest.'

Rufus groaned slightly as she leaned down and helped him with the second skate.

'Then this is going to be interesting.'

Rufus left his skates off and pushed Jess by the hips through to the great hall. He'd rolled up the rugs and pushed the furniture to the walls, leaving them with a decent-sized rink in the middle of the room, with the Christmas tree towering at the centre.

'Oh, my God,' Jess said when she saw it. 'Rufus, this is amazing. I can't believe you made me an ice rink.'

He couldn't ignore the warmth that grew in his chest at the pure delight in her voice. Really, if he could just spend the rest of his life making her happy... No. there was no place for thoughts like that. This had nothing to do with his life. This *wasn't* his life any more. He wouldn't have been able to offer this even if he'd wanted to. This wasn't his home any more. He was an interloper here now, just like her. He shook his head. This was fun. He was meant to be remembering that. Fun.

He spun Jess around, and caught her when she wobbled, her knees turning inwards as she fought for stability.

He grinned. 'Ready to try on your own?' he asked. Jess fixed an expression of determination on her face.

'Depends. Are you ready for me to skate rings around you?'

He laughed out loud.

'Come on, then. Show me what you've got.'

She pushed away from him, wobbling across the floor towards the fire, finding her balance and gliding with more and more confidence as she turned to face him. Of course she was a natural. He pushed his hands in the pockets of his jeans and leaned back against a table, not taking his eyes off her as she skated towards him, and then pinned him against the table with her hands beside his hips.

'This. Is. Amazing,' she said, punctuating each of her words with a kiss. He curled a hand to the nape of her neck, trapping her against him while he leisurely explored her mouth, only breaking off when he felt her start to slip away from him. She laughed as he caught her by the hips and pulled her back in.

'Maybe skates *weren't* such a great idea.'

'Skates were an amazing idea. Now come and race me.'

'Okay. You asked for it.' He pulled on his own skates, watching as Jess glided round the room, wobbling less and less as she found her feet.

With his boots firmly laced, he skated up beside her and reached for her hand.

'You want to race?'

Her eyes gleamed. 'I am absolutely ready to beat you. Bring it on.'

'Loser does the washing up,' he shouted as he sprinted around the tree, laughing at how much he sounded like his teenaged self. He hadn't been so...daft...for ages. Not since his dad was ill at the very least. Part of him wanted to tell himself that it was being back here, at Upton. But with a glance backwards at Jess, he wasn't sure how much he believed that now.

He stumbled as his skate caught on an uneven floorboard, but he righted himself and glided across to Jess. No wonder Jess was wobbling. Perhaps they would have been better off on the smooth kitchen tiles. But this was all worth it for the squeal of pleasure he heard from Jess as she crashed into him, narrowly avoiding a much harder meeting with the floor. Any excuse to hold her by the waist, pulling her closer until he could feel her body flush against him, her hips close, her sweet-smelling hair under his chin. He tipped her face up to his, and loved the smile that he found on her lips as he kissed into her mouth.

'I think I like how uncoordinated you are in these things,' he said, and laughed when she kicked his shin with the stopper on the front of her skate.

'I'm not uncoordinated. The floor is uneven,' she murmured, not bothering to take her mouth off his to talk. Whatever the reason, he was happy for it if it meant having her in his arms. Not that he needed an excuse. They had dispensed with those days ago. Now he could lean in and kiss her. Just like…that. For no reason other than they both wanted him to. Too soon, she was pulling away from him, skating shakily backwards as they made a circuit of the room.

'Do you know any tricks?' she asked. 'I bet you do. I want to learn.'

'Um, doing tricks your first time on rollerblades on an uneven floor is maybe not our best move,' he replied, raising his eyebrows.

'I've done so many things this week that were not the best idea that I've lost count. Now, show me or I'm just going to make it up myself.'

He heaved out a sigh and skated out backwards around the room, his feet crossing over one another as he spun around.

'I can definitely do that,' Jess declared as he came to a stop in front of her.

She pushed away on strong legs, picking up speed as she circled the room. Until she picked up one foot, tried to spin on the other and her front brake caught in a knot hole in the floorboard.

He dived to try and reach her, but he knew even before he started moving that he wasn't going to make it in time. He winced but didn't look away as she reached out to break her fall with one hand. Her yelp of pain masked the snap of bone that he was bracing himself for. He dropped to the floor beside her as she cradled her wrist against her chest. Her lower lip had disappeared between her teeth as she bit down on it. Hard.

'Oh, God, do you think it's broken?' she asked, looking up at him, her eyes wide with shock, her face pinched with pain.

He had no idea. But regardless of whether the bone was actually fractured, all he could be sure of right now was that she was in pain, and they were stranded, with no way of getting her to a hospital. All because he'd thought it would be fun to surprise her with a skating rink without properly thinking through the consequences.

'I don't know,' he said gently, putting an arm around her back, breathing out as she let her head rest on his shoulder. 'I think we should get some ice on it. Try and keep it still until we can get you to a doctor.'

He helped her up onto one of the sofas pushed back against the wall, flinching when she gasped as he helped her to stand. He pulled a blanket around her, and then knelt to unlace her boots, pulling them off and throwing them to one side, then doing the same with his own. 'I'll be back in a minute,' he said, walking quickly to the kitchen and digging round in the chest freezer for the ice pack he knew was in there somewhere.

This was all his fault. There was no way to sugar-coat it. He had been so keen to impress her that he had created a death trap of a skating rink, all the while knowing that they were trapped here without any reasonable hope of medical care.

He had been kidding himself that he could just walk away from her. He'd known, for longer than he'd admitted to himself, that he wanted more. More of what they'd shared here these past few days. Just more of *her*. And here was the cosmic payback—the reminder that he couldn't, shouldn't, be responsible for anyone but himself. When he was close to people, trying to take care of them, they got hurt. He had been on the brink of asking Jess if they could see one another after they had got out of here. But here was the reminder he needed that he shouldn't. He had needed to remember that. Remember that the thing he could do for Jess was to put some emotional distance between them. More than anything else, that was what was going to keep her safe.

He found the ice pack at last, and as he pulled it from the freezer the kitchen light flickered and went out.

'Rufus?' Jess called from the hall. 'Did you do that?'

'Another power cut,' he called, taking a torch from the pantry before he walked back through. The fire in the grate was casting light and shadow onto Jess's face, and he sat lightly beside her, careful not to jar her arm.

'Here,' he said, pressing the ice pack to her wrist, which was looking worryingly swollen. 'This will help. And these.' He handed her a couple of painkillers and a glass of water. 'How does it feel?'

'Pretty sore,' Jess said, her face still tight.

'I'm going to call 111. See if there's any chance of getting an ambulance out here.'

'You said yourself that the lane won't be passable until tomorrow.'

'But if it's broken…'

She gritted her teeth. 'Then it will still be broken tomorrow. It's okay; I can wait.'

'You were happy to call an ambulance for me,' Rufus reminded her.

'That was different and you know it. You were barely conscious and I thought you might die. This is just a sprained wrist.'

The tension in every part of her body told him that this wasn't 'just' anything.

'A broken wrist.'

'Fine, Doctor. Whatever you say,' Jess said, her voice shaky. 'But don't call. Please? It can wait until the lane is clear.'

He couldn't fight her. It wasn't fair when she was hurt. 'Okay. Tell me what you need.'

'A hug?'

Rufus exhaled. That he could do. He knew that they had to end this properly. When they left. But she needed him, and they were here now. He just had to remember that this was his fault. That this was the reason he was going to walk away. Because Jess deserved someone who could be trusted with her. Who made good decisions. Not someone who would let her get injured when they were stranded.

He eased his arms around her gently, pulling her against him, and flinching at her

sharply indrawn breath. He'd hurt her—
again. Then she relaxed into him and she
pressed a kiss to the top of her head. 'I'm
sorry,' he said into her hair. Jess looked up
at him, frowning.

'What have you got to be sorry for?'

'This was my idea. If I hadn't—'

'This was the *best*. I mean, injuries not-
withstanding, I absolutely loved it. Seriously.
Best Christmas present ever.'

He sighed. 'Yeah, well, all things considered, I'm not sure it was worth it.'

'Yeah, well, as literally the injured party
here,' Jess said, frowning 'I'm pretty sure that
this is my call, and I say it was absolutely
worth it. And I'm hurting, so you're not allowed to argue with me.'

She turned her face up for a kiss, and he
pressed his lips to hers, all the while knowing that deep down he couldn't agree with
her. This was absolutely his fault.

CHAPTER TEN

BLOODY HELL, IT HURT. For a minute she wished she hadn't been so adamant about Rufus not calling an ambulance. But she had seen that there was no way that the lane would be passable. And now that the latest painkillers were kicking in—and her second glass of red wine—it was bearable. Just. What was less bearable was the sudden distance that she felt from Rufus.

It wasn't as if in her state she was up for any sort of high jinks. And it wasn't as if he'd been anything other than perfectly attentive. He'd carried her up the stairs—despite her protestations that it was her arm that was hurt, not her legs, and she was perfectly capable of walking. He'd helped her into her pyjamas, guiding her sleeve over her swollen, bruised wrist, and wincing as if he could feel her pain himself. And then he'd leaned against the headboard, pulled her between his legs, propped her arm up on a pillow, and fallen asleep with his arms wrapped around her waist.

She'd leant into him, soaking in his warmth against the cool of the house as she watched time slip away on her phone as she waited for morning. This was their last night together. And she was spending it in his arms, with him feeling further away from her than he ever had in the time she'd known him. She shifted a little, uncomfortable, and felt Rufus's arms tighten around her. He didn't want to let her go, but he would. He had already started to. And that was what they had agreed all along. It was what they both wanted. She had known that this was how it would end. She just hadn't expected to feel it like this, with him slipping away even as he clung on to her in his sleep.

She couldn't believe that she had started to think that maybe these feeling they had for each other had a chance outside of this snowbound fairy tale. But he was the kicker. The proof that she wasn't ready. For any of this. And the proof of what she already knew, that even something that felt perfect could unravel in your hands, quicker than you were able to gather it up. At least she'd found out now. A relationship that couldn't survive a skating accident was never going to make it in the real world. It was better to know that now.

The sun gradually rose, a shard of pale light around the edges of the curtains. The alarm on her phone chimed—time for more painkillers. Thank goodness, because her wrist was throbbing. She reached for the packet on the bedside table, somehow elbowing Rufus in the stomach as she did so. He sat bolt upright, startled, jarring her wrist, until his eyes focused and then creased with concern.

'Jess, I'm so sorry. Are you okay?'

'Fine, fine,' she said as he took the packet from her, and popped the pills out of the blister pack that she'd been struggling with.

'So…do you think the roads are clear?' she asked. If this thing was over, there was no point in dragging it out. It was clear that Rufus wanted it done, and if he was out already, there was no point in sticking around. She knew where that led. Suddenly she was grateful for the lesson her parents had taught her. Sticking around once the light had gone out only made things worse.

She scooted out of bed, swallowed her painkillers with a gulp of water and crossed over to the window, hugging her arm to her chest.

Pulling back the curtains, she started at the unfamiliar view. Great swathes of snow had melted, leaving their snowmen stranded in a sea of grass, a reminder of a time when things between them had been full of promise. Well, there was no point thinking about that now. The sun was up. Yesterday was over. Christmas was over. It was time to get back to real life. And the sooner the better. She flashed back to yesterday morning, watching the ice melt, safe in Rufus's arms. Well, not today.

'Snow's gone,' she said, turning to look back at him.

'That's great,' he said, standing up.

No need to sound quite *so enthusiastic.*

'I meant because we can get your arm seen to…' So something of what she had been thinking must have shown on her face.

'Of course.' She pulled on a jumper, wincing as she pushed her arm through the sleeve, but brushing off Rufus's offer of help. It took less than an hour for them to pack her things, and then the door was locked, Rufus threw her bag in the boot of her rental four-by-four and they were crunching across the driveway, Upton Manor growing ever smaller in the wing mirror, until they rounded a corner of the lane and it disappeared completely.

CHAPTER ELEVEN

'YOU DON'T HAVE to stay.'

The emergency department in the hospital Rufus had driven to was overflowing with patients sitting on piles of coats in the waiting room, and trolleys lined up against any available wall space. The nurse who'd triaged her had warned them that they were in for a long wait.

'I'm not leaving you here alone,' Rufus argued, frowning.

But she couldn't do this. Couldn't pretend things between them were still normal now that they had left Upton. 'I won't be alone. I messaged Lara, let her know what was going on. They finally scheduled a flight and she'll be here by this afternoon.'

He watched her for several long moments, the harsh fluorescent lighting throwing deep shadows beneath his eyes. 'So that's it? I'm dismissed?'

She creased her brow. She thought he'd be pleased to be let off the hook—now he was angry with her?

'It's not like that. We both said that this would be over once we were away from Upton Manor. I know you want it to be. So there's no need to stick around out of some sense of… I don't know. Duty, I guess.'

The lines between his eyebrows deepened. 'You think that's why I'm here? Duty?'

'Isn't it?' she asked, not sure she wanted to know what his answer would be.

'I'm here because I want to see that you're okay. Just because things aren't going to carry on between us doesn't mean that I don't care.'

Jess huffed: she didn't understand why he was making this so hard. She thought that she was giving him what he wanted. What he'd said he wanted. 'Actually,' she said, 'I'm pretty sure that is what it means. Or at least that you don't want to care.'

'Are you saying you don't care for me? That you would go, if the situation was reversed?'

She shook her head. 'Of course not, but—'

'So do me a favour and give me a little credit.'

Ouch. She'd forgotten just how grouchy Rufus could be. He'd softened, so slowly she hadn't noticed it in the days that they'd been together. And now he was back, the block of ice that had fallen through the front door of Upton Manor two days before Christmas. Well, she needed him even less than she needed the Rufus she'd gone to bed and woken up with, and she had no qualms about kicking him out on his ear.

'Seriously, Rufus. I've got a long wait ahead of me. I'm in pain, and I just want to put my headphones in and zone out until they can see me. This is me letting you off the hook. Honestly, you should go. I want you to go. Please?' She didn't have the energy for this. Her body didn't have the capacity to deal with her heart breaking as well as her wrist. She needed to pretend that she didn't feel any of this, and she couldn't do that with him sitting beside her, being more…just *more* than she'd ever thought he would be.

'We're breaking up in a hospital emergency department?' he asked.

That caught her attention. 'Breaking up? We were never together. We never wanted that. This is what we agreed all along.' This was why she needed him to go. She could barely think straight right now, never mind explain how she was feeling. This was all too much.

'I know, but… I just didn't see it ending here. Like this.'

And there he went, proving her point entirely, and reminding her of why she'd told herself all along that she didn't want to make this work. 'Well, what have I been saying all this time? That's how it happens. You think everything is fine and then something happens and it's not any more.'

Rufus leaned forward, his elbows resting on spread knees, and his eyes fixed on the floor as he took several deep breaths. Eventually he looked up, fixed her with an intense stare. 'Can I at least call you? Check that you're okay?' He held her gaze, refused to break eye contact with her, so that she was the one who had to look away. Those painkillers were doing nothing for the tearing pain in her chest. She needed him to walk away before she changed her mind, begged him to stay and made a huge mistake.

'Yes, okay. You can call. But, Rufus, please just…just go.'

Lara burst through the doors three hours later and swept Jess into a huge hug, only loosening her grip when Jess squealed and reminded her about the probably broken wrist currently trapped between them.

'You silly thing—how did this happen?' Lara asked. 'I wasn't worried when the photos stopped because I assumed you were making the most of being bunked up with Rufus. Where is he, anyway?' She looked around the waiting room, as if she expected him to pop up from behind a row of chairs or something.

'Oh. I asked him to go.'

Lara gaped at her, her mouth and eyes wide. 'And he actually went?'

'Yes! I wanted him to. I didn't give him a choice.'

'Um, *why*?' Lara asked, still looking at her as if she was missing several important cognitive functions. 'Seriously. Am I missing something here? Was I deluding myself thinking that you guys got it together?'

Jess sighed, slouching into the back-breaking chair. How long had she been here now? How long since Rufus had walked away? Since she'd pushed him away?

'It was nothing,' she lied. 'Just passing the time until the snow cleared.'

Lara crossed her arms and fixed her with a look. 'You know lying to me doesn't work.

Not even when you're at your best. And you're seriously not at your best just now. How's the arm?'

'Really bloody painful, now that you ask,' Jess said, trying to force a laugh.

'I'm sorry. We don't have to talk about Rufus if you're not ready. But we can whenever you are.'

Jess nodded. 'Great, let's pencil that in for *never*, shall we?'

'It worked, you know. Upton Manor's engagement is through the roof. It's going to be fully booked all year, and I have this friend who does location-scouting for a movie production company... Never mind. I'll tell you about that later. My followers loved you, as always. And Rufus. You looked really good together. It was...fairy tale.'

'Precisely. Fairy tale, as in "not real". And possibly cursed,' Jess said, letting her black mood show. 'It was fun, but it's over, and I'm not ready to talk about it.'

'Okay,' Lara said at last, drawing Jess close with an arm around her shoulders and planting a big kiss on the side of her head. 'So what's going on with the doctors? Did they give you the good drugs yet?'

CHAPTER TWELVE

RUFUS GLANCED AT his phone for the thousandth time that morning. He'd muted his Instagram notifications because he just couldn't keep up with them. Jess had been right. Lara had worked her magic—even from a different country. But his feed was so full of Jess that he couldn't bear to look at it—never mind like, comment and share. He knew he needed to do it, but he couldn't. Not yet. Not when so many of those comments were asking what the deal was with the two of them, and he didn't know how to answer.

No, that wasn't true. He knew what was going on. They were over. It had all melted away with the snow. Just how they'd agreed. The problem was that he didn't like it. He wanted…he wanted *her*. It was as simple as that. He needed her. But nothing had changed. None of the reasons he knew she'd be better off without him.

And so he was here, in his parents' house, mainlining Twiglets and avoiding mince pies, and trying to answer his family's questions about how he'd spent his Christmas without touching on anything X-rated. Or showing the gaping hole that seemed to be growing in his chest since Jess had kicked him out of the hospital. He should just pick up the phone and call her. Just to make sure she was okay. To make sure that Lara had turned up and she wasn't still stuck alone in a corridor somewhere.

But Jess didn't need him.

So why couldn't he stop thinking about her?

'A watched phone never rings, love.'

He rolled his eyes at his mam. She'd been dropping hints, getting less and less subtle since the minute she'd arrived at the hospital to pick him up, eyes equal parts concern and curiosity. Once he'd assured her that he was okay—the call to the same hospital they'd been summoned to when his dad had suffered his heart attack wasn't an ideal Christmas present—he'd known that she could see that something had happened.

'You know you can tell me about it, don't

you?' she said, pressing gently on what she must have known was a sore spot.

'About what?' Playing dumb was the only weapon he had, and he knew that it was nothing against his mother's arsenal.

'About whatever it is that happened that's got you looking so sad. About why you're stuck here all glum, instead of being wherever Jess is right now, trying to work out whatever's happened.'

'Nothing's happened, Mam. I keep telling you. She lives down there. I'm here. We enjoyed getting to know each other for a few days, and now we've gone back to our own lives. It's what we both wanted. Want.'

'Well, call me interfering—'

'You're interf—'

'But, love, you don't look like someone who's got what they want. You look like someone trying to come to terms with losing someone.'

He crossed his arms. There was no point having this conversation. It wasn't going to change anything. 'Even if I wanted—'

'Which you clearly do.'

'Even if I wanted things to be different, we don't always get what we want. What would be the point of saying that I want Jess? That

I want to see her again because I think I'm falling for her? That I see myself building a life with her? Some people just aren't meant for that. Shouldn't have other people relying on them.'

His mam creased her eyebrows together thoughtfully. 'Why do I get the feeling we're not just talking about Jess here?'

'We are.' He huffed. 'And we're not, I suppose. It was my fault that you and Dad had to leave Upton. My fault that he's heartbroken about it.'

She scoffed. 'His heart was already broken. I've got the cardiologist's report to prove it. But you're right—it was Upton Manor that did it. It was trying to take responsibility for the family without accepting help. Without talking to me. Without being willing to compromise. Because I would have gladly gone years before we did if I'd known how bad things had got. If I'd been able to spare us your dad's heart attack. Don't repeat his mistakes, please, Rufus. Why don't you try sharing the problem? What's stopping you?'

Jess flicked through the TV guide, trying to find something in there that would make the hinterland between Christmas and New Year feel slightly less like the *Twilight Zone*. But it was either a Disney movie or sixties sitcom reruns, neither of which were going to work for her current melancholic state of mind. The initial flurry of excitement when she'd arrived home had fizzled in the twenty-four hours since she'd been back.

Lara had offered to take her straight back to her flat in Oxford, but she wanted to finish the conversation she'd started with her mum on Christmas Day. And it had gone better than she had thought. She'd offered to go to family therapy with her mum and dad. Or grief counselling. Or *anything* that would crack through the icy silence of her childhood home.

She'd made the error of checking her email. To find the job offer that had been made at the conference waiting for her in writing. If she took it, she'd be working a half-hour drive from Upton Manor. If she wanted to give this thing with Rufus a shot, there was nothing practical stopping her. Nothing at all in her way other than the fear that one day, without warning, her life would descend to the same level of sadness that she was currently soaking in at her parents' house. She looked up as her mum cleared her throat, standing in the door-frame, coat on and handbag over her shoulder.

'Will you be all right if we nip out for an hour?'

'It's just a broken wrist, Mum. Where are you off to?'

Her dad appeared behind her mum, and Jess didn't recognise the look that passed between them.

'We thought about what you said, on the phone, about talking to someone, and we managed to get an appointment. I don't know if it will…'

Jess launched herself off the sofa and wrapped her mum in a hug. 'Thank you,' she mumbled, the words almost lost in her mum's scarf.

She pulled herself upright and took a deep breath. 'I'm so happy that you're doing this,' she told her parents. 'And I really, really hope it helps you to be happy.'

Her mum gave an awkward smile. 'Well,' she said, 'that's all we want for you, too.'

After all these years, they had decided that what they had was still worth fighting for.

She could do that. She could fight. Even if it didn't work, even if it was too late, she could choose to fight, rather than hide out of fear of failure.

She was left with only one question on her mind—what was the fastest way to get to Yorkshire with only one functional arm? Would Lara drive her three hundred miles north just two days after she'd done the exact same journey in reverse? And then helpfully make herself scarce so that she could have this thing out with Rufus? Was that even what he wanted?

Sure, he had seemed hurt when she'd asked him to leave—but she'd done it because she'd felt him pulling away. So…what? She'd torched the thing to the ground rather than have a grown-up conversation about her feelings. Maybe she was more her parents' daughter than she thought. But she wasn't going to accept that she couldn't change her behaviour. She had a choice about whether she wanted to make her future, or just have it happen to her. And she was going to choose the option that at least had the possibility of Rufus in there.

She was digging in the sofa cushions, looking for her phone to call Lara and ask for the mother of all favours, when she heard her mum talking to someone in the driveway. Probably something that she'd ordered online in the sales, hoping that some retail therapy would fill the new Rufus-shaped hole in her life. She carried on looking for her phone.

'Jess...'

She spun on the spot, to find that the doorway was filled with Rufus, and she clutched the sofa cushion to her stomach. 'What are you doing here?' she asked. Was this real? Was he here because he wanted her? Because he wanted to try and make this thing work? Or was it something else?

He did something with his face, and she couldn't decide whether it was more smile or grimace.

'Talk to me, Rufus. I'm losing my mind here, imagining things. Did I leave something behind at Upton Manor? Is this a lost property thing?'

'I... I don't know what kind of thing this is. Other than a *I couldn't bear waiting another minute to see you* thing. Is it okay? That I'm here?'

She was slightly breathless, but she couldn't quite believe that this was real. She nodded, hesitantly.

'I'm not sure I should be doing this' he said.

'I told myself I shouldn't be doing this. I don't know if I can make you happy. If I can keep you that way.'

'No one can see into the future.'

'And you're suddenly okay about that?'

'No. But my mum and dad just left for marriage counselling. They decided they still want to work at what they have. It's hard not to be impressed by their example.'

'And if I mess up? I want to look after you.'

'I don't need looking after. And what if I mess up? We work at it, if we think it's worth it. Do you? Think it's worth it? Are you willing to try?'

'You know I am. I'm here.'

He smiled—definitely a smile—and she felt her heart physically swell with anticipation. 'I think this is an *I'm falling in love with you* thing,' he said. And she thought her heart might actually burst. 'An *I can't believe we've been so stupid* thing.'

She dropped the cushion, and he frowned as his eyes followed it to the floor.

'What the heck are you doing to the sofa?'

'Looking for my phone,' Jess said, as if it was the most normal thing in the world. 'I needed to call Lara. It was urgent.' He was by her side in a second, his hand disappearing down the back of the sofa and re-emerging a moment later with her phone.

He held it out to her, but she didn't take it from him. Instead, she just smiled. 'I don't think I need it now.'

'You said it was urgent.'

'It was. I needed Lara to drive me. To you. But you're here.'

He took a step closer, and his hands dropped to her hips. Bending his head, he caught her eye. 'And what were you going to say when you got there?'

'Well, I was thinking about telling you that I was an idiot to make you leave. And I'm sorry. And can we talk about what we want and what we're both scared of? And maybe being grown-ups about this relationship that we seem to be having?'

She was madly in love with every single one of the lines that appeared around his eyes as he smiled at her. 'Okay. Well, I think I would have liked it if you'd turned up on my doorstep and told me all that. Maybe you could tell me all of it here instead.'

'Instead you turned up on mine. And told me you're falling for me.' She looped her good arm around his neck, reached up on tiptoe, and pulled herself a little higher.

'So what does this "being an adult" thing entail?' he asked, his voice a murmur.

'I think telling me you're falling in love with me was a good start.'

'Yeah?'

'Yeah. I'm thinking of trying it out.'

His lips curled into a smile. 'I think I might like that. When you're ready. And if you're not, we'll talk. There's nothing that we can't deal with if we talk. And if I'm going to spend half my life on the motorway so that we can do that face to face I don't care. I'm still in. It broke me to walk away from you thinking I wasn't going to see you again. I never want to feel like that again.'

She brushed a kiss against the corner of his mouth. 'So if I told you that I had a job offer from the university, and I was thinking of taking it, you wouldn't think I was jumping the gun?'

'I think that would be just about the best thing that I'd heard all year. I'd beg you to take it. To give me a chance. To give *us* a chance.'

'Okay,' she said on an out-breath. 'Okay, then. I'll take it. I'll take you. I'll take everything.'

EPILOGUE

THERE REALLY WERE an ungodly number of buttons on this dress.

She fidgeted as Lara fastened them up her spine, and she twitched at her lace sleeve.

'Stand still,' Lara said, flicking her spine with a finger, 'or this is never going to end.'

'Ow, that hurt.'

'Good. Now stand still.'

Jess looked down at her wedding dress, the same one she had tried on her first Christmas at Upton, and smiled. As if she could even think about wearing anything else to marry Rufus.

The past year had seen changes at Upton— film crews, back-to-back bookings, a subtle but steady climb in the bank balance. And it had never looked more beautiful than it did this morning, decorated in holly and mistletoe, fires burning, candles everywhere. Just as it had the first time that she'd seen it.

And then the dress was finally fastened and her hair was perfect and Lara was handing her a bouquet, and she couldn't believe that she was really doing this.

Marriage had looked like a trap her entire life, until she'd met Rufus and he'd made it feel like an adventure. And her parents, who had seemed so entombed by matrimony, had decided that it was worth fighting after all, and her whole worldview had been tipped upside down and thoroughly shaken.

The constant, throughout, had been Rufus.

And there he was, waiting for her at the bottom of the staircase as she stepped carefully down, his reddish-brown curls temporarily tamed, a sprig of holly in the buttonhole of his suit jacket. A far cry from the half-dead man she'd dragged over the threshold a year ago.

'You look beautiful,' he said as she reached him, leaning in for a kiss before they'd even started on their vows.

She glanced over at her parents, still working. Still fighting for one another, even after everything had seemed so bleak. And Rufus's parents, who had never faltered in their love for one another, even when they had faced the worst.

It turned out getting married was shockingly easy. *Repeat after me. Sign here. Smile there.* And then it was for ever—her and Rufus. Looking after one another. Looking after Upton. Bringing their families together. Fighting for each other.

For ever.

* * * * *

*If you enjoyed this story,
check out these other great reads from
Ellie Darkins*

Reunited by the Tycoon's Twins
Falling Again for Her Island Fling
Surprise Baby for the Heir
Conveniently Engaged to the Boss

All available now!